# Drumshee Timeline Series
## Book 4

Cora Harrison taught primary-school children in England for twenty-five years before moving to a small farm in Kilfenora, Co. Clare. The farm includes an Iron Age fort, with the remains of a small castle inside it, and the mysterious atmosphere of this ancient place gave Cora the idea for a series of historical novels tracing the survival of the ringfort through the centuries. *The Secret of 1798* follows *Nuala & her Secret Wolf*, *The Secret of the Seven Crosses* and *The Secret of Drumshee Castle* in the Drumshee Timeline Series.

*For Caitriona Malone, Amy Roche, Michelle Roche*
*and all the children of Inchovea School*

## OTHER TITLES BY CORA HARRISON

*Nuala & her Secret Wolf*
Drumshee Timeline Series Book 1

*The Secret of the Seven Crosses*
Drumshee Timeline Series Book 2

*The Secret of Drumshee Castle*
Drumshee Timeline Series Book 3

*The Famine Secret*
Drumshee Timeline Series Book 5

# The Secret of 1798

## Drumshee Timeline Series
## Book 4

### Cora Harrison

*Illustrated by Orla Roche*

WOLFHOUND PRESS

First published in 1998 by
Wolfhound Press Ltd
68 Mountjoy Square
Dublin 1, Ireland
Tel: (353-1) 874 0354
Fax: (353-1) 872 0207

Wolfhound Press receives financial assistance from the Arts Council/ An Chomhairle Ealaíon, Dublin, Ireland.

British Library Cataloguing in Publication Data
A catalogue record for this book is available from the British Library.

ISBN 0-86327-638-5

10 9 8 7 6 5 4

Cover illustration: Orla Roche
Cover Design: Estresso
Typesetting: Wolfhound Press
Printed and bound by The Guernsey Press Co. Ltd, Guernsey, Channel Islands

# CHAPTER ONE

𝕱or ever afterwards, Caitriona would hear 1798 described as 'the year the French came'; but for her it was always the year that the dog came.

And yet it wasn't much of a dog when she saw it first — more like a lump of wet flesh and clotted hair; but from that first moment, the brown eyes were soft and loving and the long tail beat a frantic tattoo.

Caitriona first saw the little dog when she was fishing in the River Fergus at Drumshee, her father's farm, one damp day in February. In the summer there were plenty of small trout in the river, but on that winter day it was just a way of escaping from all the housework which her stepmother loaded on her; an excuse to sit and dream and hum her favourite songs softly to herself.

The little river was flowing fast and furiously, and Caitriona's eyes were on the eddying circles around a rock under the stone bridge — or is it a rock? she thought. Surely I'd have noticed it before? She dropped her fishing rod and went to investigate, and that was the first time she saw Bess.

When Caitriona pulled the puppy out of the river and freed her from the sack in which she had been dumped into the water, Bess was more dead than alive.

'Oh, you poor little thing!' said Caitriona. She took her shawl from around her shoulders, and rubbed the soaking little body until life and warmth returned to it. And then the pink tongue came out and licked her hand, the long tail wagged, and the soft eyes fixed on Caitriona with a look of love which was never to disappear while Bess had breath in her body.

But at that moment the dog seemed to have very little chance of life. She was painfully thin; Caitriona could see every rib standing out through the wet fur. What can I do with her? thought Caitriona.

Her family were very poor. They had never gone hungry yet, but at twelve Caitriona was old enough to know that life was a constant struggle for her parents. Still, she thought, this is a very small dog; she won't want all that much to eat. And she'll help to protect the new lambs from getting lost or being stolen by foxes.

Vigorously rubbing the little body, Caitriona began to make plans. First she would get her father on her side. She was his pet and could usually twist him around her little finger. If he said the dog could stay, then her stepmother would have to agree.

Still carrying the puppy, Caitriona made her way along the hedge around the river meadows. She skirted the bottom of the little hill on which she lived, keeping well away from the house and from her stepmother's eye.

By the time she reached the Big Meadow, the puppy had fallen fast asleep. Warm, dry, and comforted, she lay snuggled into Caitriona's shoulder. Already Caitriona loved her passionately. She could not think what she would do if her father refused to keep the dog.

Caitriona's father was walking around the meadow checking each of their four cows, gently passing his hands over them and talking soothingly to them. Caitriona watched him anxiously. She knew what he was doing. He was trying to see if the cows were in calf. Without calves, there would be no milk, no calf to sell, and no spare money for the family.

The wind had risen, and it blew a sound towards her. Tom McMahon was singing to himself, a low rich sound, a tune that Caitriona did not know; but she knew instantly what it meant. Her father was happy, and that must mean that the cows were all in calf.

Moving cautiously, so as not to scare the cows, Caitriona approached him, smiling sweetly.

'What's that song you're singing, Da?' she asked.

Her father ignored the question. His eyes were fixed on the bundle in her arms.

'What in the name of glory have you there?' he asked.

Caitriona hesitated, and then decided on a desperate gamble. She knew how soft-hearted her father was about animals.

'It's a poor little puppy dog,' she said, in a voice which trembled slightly. 'Someone threw her into the river and tried to drown her. She was tied up in a sack.'

She held out the bundle to her father and he took it reluctantly. The dog woke and gave a whimper at finding itself abandoned — and then the pink tongue came out and licked Tom's face, and the skinny tail wagged feebly .

Tom's eyes softened. 'Poor little thing,' he said. 'She's half-starved as well as half-drowned.'

Caitriona held her breath. The battle was half-won already, she knew. Her father was stroking the damp, warm fur and the dog was licking his hands, wriggling her little body in a frenzy of love and desire to please.

'What are you going to do with it?' asked Tom, handing the puppy back to Caitriona.

'Could I keep her, Da?'

Her father tried to look stern. 'Caitriona, you know what your stepmother would say to that. There's hardly enough food for ourselves, never mind for every stray dog that passes the place.'

'Yes, I know, Da,' said Caitriona humbly. She wasn't really worried. They never did go hungry. There were only two children in the family, just herself and little Michael, who was ten years younger than she; they were not like other families around, which had ten or twelve children to feed. In any case, she knew from the way her father had handled the puppy that he would not drown it.

'Well, the two goats have just kidded and they both have plenty of milk,' said Tom slowly. 'I don't suppose they'd miss a few cupfuls for this poor little thing.'

Caitriona's heart began to beat quickly with joy, but she controlled her excitement. It was not unknown for her stepmother to make Tom change his mind.

'Come up to the house with me, Da,' she pleaded. 'You can tell Ma all about the dog.'

Her father tried to hide a smile. 'And who's going to do the work while I'm trying to argue your stepmother into this piece of foolishness?' he asked.

'It's going to rain,' said Caitriona. 'You can have a sup of buttermilk and a little rest, and you can teach me that new song you were singing. Did you learn it at the cattle fair?'

'Where else?' said her father. 'Listen now — I'll hum it and you see if you can pick up the tune, and then I'll teach you the words.'

They walked slowly up the Big Meadow, across the lane and up the Togher Field; by the time they reached the cattle drinking place, Caitriona had learned the new song. Both she and her father were great singers. They sang all the old songs, day in and day out, but it was lovely to have a brand-new one. The puppy seemed to enjoy the song too; her soft brown eyes stared earnestly into Caitriona's blue ones, and she seemed to be listening to every note.

As they crossed the cabbage garden, Tom stopped

in the middle of a verse. Down in front of the little whitewashed cottage Caitriona could see the thin, energetic figure of her stepmother bustling about, carrying food to the pig and talking to two-year-old Michael.

'You take the puppy into that old cabin,' Tom said softly. 'There's plenty of straw there and you can make her a bed. Stay with her for a while; give me a chance to talk to your Ma on my own.'

Caitriona crept quietly into the little stone cabin beside her house. There was plenty of straw, as her father had said, and she did make a bed for the little dog; but it was reluctant to leave the warmth and comfort of her arms, so she sat on the straw, nursing the puppy and wondering what her stepmother would say.

The trouble with Ma, Caitriona thought, is that you never really know. It all depends on her mood. Everything seemed very quiet at the moment, anyway. That probably meant that Caitriona's stepmother was listening to what her husband was saying, rather than rushing out straight away and demanding that Caitriona get rid of the dog. I'll count up to a hundred, Caitriona thought, and if she doesn't come out until after that, it will be a sign of good luck.

She had got to ninety-two when she heard the door of the farmhouse open. Quickly she rushed through the other numbers, determined to have them finished in time, and she had just said 'one hundred' when her father came to the doorway. Behind him was Ann McMahon, with Michael by the hand. Caitriona held her breath. It was hard to see her stepmother's face in the dim light, but what she could see was not very hopeful. The thin lips were set in a grim line.

Michael saved the situation: he toddled forward to see this new animal, stumbled on a piece of stone lying on the ground and began to wail. Ann started forward, but the dog was quicker. In a flash she was out of Caitriona's lap and standing over the sobbing Michael, licking his face. Michael sat up; the wailing stopped abruptly, and he put his fat little arms around the dog's neck.

'Do you like the little doggie, Michael?' said Caitriona quickly.

Michael nodded. 'Nice doggie,' he announced obediently, and put his cheek against the puppy's face. 'What doggie name?' he enquired, after an unsuccessful attempt to stop the dog's tail from wagging.

'She's called Bess,' said Caitriona quickly, with an eye on her stepmother. Surely no one could condemn to death a dog who already had a name?

To her great relief, she could see that Ann was beginning to smile as she looked at the little boy with the puppy in his arms. It could not have happened better. Michael was his mother's darling — the only child who had lived, after the deaths of so many others; the only boy of the family.

'Well, if we must have this dog, Caitriona, you're going to have to look after it,' said Ann grimly. 'And it's not to come in the house, ever. I'm not going to have it dirtying my floor with its muddy feet.'

Caitriona nodded silently. She had not expected anything else. She had never known anyone to set such store by cleanliness as her stepmother did. The house was limewashed inside and out at least three times a year, the stone flags on the kitchen floor were scrubbed daily, and you could almost see your face in the copper saucepans. Bess would be better off outside. She would be warm and comfortable in the little cabin.

A quiver of joy ran through Caitriona at the thought of having a dog of her own. She knelt down beside Michael and put her arms about the dog and the child, loving them both with such intensity that it almost hurt.

# CHAPTER TWO

All went well for the next month or so. Ann McMahon tolerated Bess, while Michael continued to worship her. In fact, though Ann would not admit it, she had never had so easy a time with him: Michael trotted after Bess all day long, while his mother swept and scrubbed and dusted to her heart's content.

Bess loved Michael, but Caitriona was her favourite. If Caitriona had to do housework, Bess waited quietly outside the door until she had finished; and wherever Caitriona went on the farm, Bess was beside her, tail wagging.

No one had much idea of how old Bess was, but she grew very fast, even on the few scraps of food that Caitriona managed to get for her. Soon the little dog had filled out and her coat had become thick and glossy. She had silky ears which fell on either side of her face like ringlets, a softly-waving black and white coat, and a long tail fringed like a plume. Caitriona thought Bess was the loveliest dog she had ever seen.

She was very useful, also. Caitriona discovered this one evening in May. It was Caitriona's job to shut up the hens, geese and ducks every night, before she had her supper. Some evenings it went well, but on other evenings the ducks turned stubborn and ran here, there, and everywhere except into their cabin. They could not be left outside or they would be eaten by foxes before morning. When Caitriona was by herself, sometimes she spent half an hour chasing them around.

That evening, however, after Bess had watched for a few minutes, she knew exactly what to do: she walked quietly behind the ducks, driving them steadily ahead of her, while Caitriona held the cabin door open and stopped them going off to the side.

'You were quick this evening,' commented her stepmother when she came in.

'Bess helped me,' said Caitriona smugly.

Ann sniffed but said nothing. She was concentrating on draining the water from the potatoes. Caitriona placed on the table the willow basket which her father had woven; Ann tipped the drained potatoes into it, and Caitriona took the pot of buttermilk from the north windowsill and set it on the table. That would be their evening meal: potatoes and buttermilk, and a little bacon from the side that hung from the kitchen rafters.

I'm sick of bacon, thought Caitriona. She did not dare say anything or her stepmother would give her a lecture about how much better off she was than other girls around Drumshee, but she silently resolved to go fishing the next day. Fish would make a nice change, and now, in May, was the best time to catch trout. I won't say anything tonight, she decided; I can ask Da in the morning, after I've finished my jobs in the house.

She looked at her father affectionately. He was so easy-going and kind ... Sometimes she wondered what their lives would have been like if he had not married Ann when Caitriona was four years old.

Caitriona could not really remember her own mother very well, but she was sure that she would have been very different from Ann.

'Da,' she said aloud, 'you should have seen Bess today! She helped me shut the ducks up for the night. You know how easily frightened they are? Well, she crept along behind them, and when they fluttered she stopped still and waited, and then just moved on again. We got them shut up in double-quick time.'

Tom looked interested. 'Is that so?' he said. 'We might try her with sheep, soon. She'd be a great help to me if she could drive them.'

'Take care she doesn't attack any of them,' said his wife sourly. 'We haven't got many as it is, what with the bad lambing this winter. You don't want to lose any more.'

'Oh, she won't do that,' said Tom easily. 'She's very good with all the other animals. Caitriona has trained her well.'

Caitriona smiled with pleasure. 'I'll practise with her after I've finished my supper, if you like,' she offered.

'Oh, no, you won't,' said Ann. 'We're going to visit the Quins after supper — and don't let us have any of your nonsense about not wanting to sing for them, either. You'll sing if you are asked to.'

Caitriona scowled. Usually she loved to sing — she sang all day around the farm, she sang in church, she sang for all the neighbours — but she hated to sing for old Mr Quin. He was such a critical old man, always making her go over notes again and again until they sounded just right to him.

'Don't worry about Bess for now,' broke in Tom hastily. 'Just keep letting her practise on the ducks. She's a bit young for sheep yet. Sure, anyway, if she can manage ducks, she can manage anything.'

Caitriona smiled to herself. Her father always did want to keep the peace between her and her stepmother, but tonight he was especially anxious that Caitriona should be in a good mood. He was very proud of her singing, and old Pat Quin was the finest musician in the parish — in the whole of County Clare, some people said. Tom wanted to make sure that Caitriona learned all that she could from the old man.

It was a good evening, after all. For once Mr Quin did not interrupt Caitriona, and when she finished her song his eyes were filled with tears.

'She's wasted here entirely,' he said to Tom. 'With a voice like that she should be off in London or Paris, getting it trained.'

Tom laughed good-naturedly.

'Well, I don't see myself getting the money to send her to Paris,' he said, 'so she'll just have to go on singing in Drumshee and giving us all the pleasure of listening to her.'

Caitriona glowed with pleasure. It was not often that she got praised like this. She could see how pleased her father was, and even her stepmother was smiling.

As soon as Caitriona got home she rushed into the little cabin where Bess was kept. Gathering the puppy into her arms, she said, 'Wouldn't it be wonderful to go to Paris and be trained as a singer, Bess! You could go too. We'd go on one of those big ships

that we sometimes meet when we're out fishing ....
Imagine it, Bess! I might be a famous singer!'

Bess licked her face encouragingly, but Caitriona
suddenly started to laugh at herself. It was too much
to imagine. It was very unlikely that she would sing
in any place farther away than Kilfenora, the little
village three miles from Drumshee.

'Anyway, Bess,' she said, 'you and I will go fishing
tomorrow.'

The next day was a glorious one, with not a cloud
in the sky and the crab-apple blossom pink against
the intensity of blue. For once, Ann was in a good
mood, so at the breakfast table Caitriona dared to
bring up the subject of fishing. To her surprise, her
stepmother not only agreed, but provided a basket
with some buttermilk and a few hunks of soda bread
for Caitriona's lunch.

'Take care,' said Tom as she went off. 'The river is
deep, and it's flowing very strongly just now. Don't
fall in. We don't want to lose our singing bird.'

Caitriona laughed. She knew that her father was
only half-serious. She was an excellent swimmer. He
had taught her himself when she was only three
years old, and every year, when he made his summer
trips to the sea — catching sea-fish, or fetching sea-
weed to fertilise the potatoes — she had gone with
him and swum in the cold, turbulent Atlantic Ocean.

Thinking about this, Caitriona decided to go to
the place which her father called 'Caitriona's
swimming hole' — the still, dark little pool, at a place
where the river curved around a bank of stone,
where she had leaned to swim when she was little. It
would be a good place for the trout. She whistled to

Bess and they set off together, down the steep slope of the meadow, through the gap in the hedge, and down the river meadows.

At the pool, Caitriona sat on a clump of heather and attached a hook to the string on her hazel rod. She carefully tied on the imitation fly which she had made from one of the ducks' feathers and, with a quick flick of her strong wrist, let it skim the water's surface. No luck. She tried again, and this time she felt a tug.

She held her breath. For a little while she thought she would lose the trout — the current was carrying it away too fast — but she moved her rod steadily in the way that her father had taught her, and in a minute she had landed it .

Not too big, but enough for a meal for one at least. Already Caitriona could almost taste it, fried in a little butter and stuffed with the lemon-balm which grew outside the back door. Carefully she detached it from the hook, knocked it on a stone and covered it with some big leaves from the marsh irises which grew nearby. Then she tried again. It was half an hour before she caught another, but then she caught two in quick succession.

'Now one for Michael,' she said to Bess, who was sitting patiently by her side watching the rod making a gleaming arc through the air.

At the word 'Michael', Bess pricked up her long silky ears and looked up towards the house on the hilltop. She seemed a little uneasy.

'He's too young to come fishing,' explained Caitriona.

Bess continued to look uneasy. She stood up and

took an uncertain step back.

'Sit down, Bess,' whispered Caitriona sharply. She could feel a nibble on her line.

For the first time in her life, Bess disobeyed her. She shot up the field, running as fast as she could, catapulting her small body through the gap in the hedge.

I suppose she heard Michael calling her, thought Caitriona, feeling rather annoyed. The line was slack; she had lost the fish. She pulled in her line, tied on a different fly and once again let it snake across the water. Nothing happened. She was determined that Michael should have a fish of his very own, not just a bit from hers or Ann's, so again and again she tried.

She could hear Bess barking somewhere. Caitriona listened, puzzled. Bess was not much of a barker, unless there was a reason for it, but now she was barking harder than she ever had before. Caitriona put down her rod reluctantly.

Then she heard her stepmother scream her name, in what sounded like a frenzy of fear.

'Caitriona!' came the shrill sound; and then, 'Tom! Help me! Tom, the dog has gone mad! Come quickly — you'll have to kill it — it might have rabies!'

Caitriona tore up the hill, her mouth dry with fear. Rabies was a terrible disease which made dogs mad; anyone who was bitten by a dog with rabies would die also. Only the week before, a mad dog in Corofin had been shot in the main street by the soldiers, while everyone else stayed behind closed doors.

By the time Caitriona reached the yard in front of the house, she was soaked in sweat and her knees were trembling.

Bess was barking into Ann's face, trying to catch her long skirt in her teeth, while the terrified woman aimed blows at the dog with her long-handled broom.

At the first sight of Bess, Caitriona's fear left her. The dog was certainly not mad. She dashed over, seized Bess by the scruff of the neck and pulled her away. Bess, however, started to bark into Caitriona's face. Caitriona was not afraid, but she was puzzled. It was almost as if Bess was trying to tell her something.

At that moment Tom came running up the long avenue, with his spade in his hand. He had been earthing up the young potatoes in the Big Meadow, and had heard the noise .

His wife rounded on him quickly. 'That dog is mad!' she screamed. 'She tried to attack me, and now she's trying to attack Caitriona. Kill her quickly!'

'No!' shouted Caitriona. 'She's not mad, Da. Look at her. She's just trying to tell me something.'

Tom looked carefully at the dog. 'She doesn't have rabies, anyway,' he said to his wife. 'I've seen a dog with rabies, and they foam at the mouth. Look at her eyes, too — they're quite sane. A mad dog has a staring eye. You'd know it straight away. Has anything happened to her, Caitriona?'

'I don't know, Da,' said Caitriona, trying vainly to quieten the hysterically-barking dog. 'She just left me when we were fishing and came up here.'

'I saw her pass the house,' said Ann. 'She ran straight past me and went up through the cabbage garden, and then she came back a few minutes later and started this.'

'Where's Michael?' said Caitriona suddenly.

'Asleep in his bed.'

'He can't be, with all this noise.'

Without answering, Ann dashed inside, followed by Tom and Caitriona — and by Bess, who, for the first time ever, dared to come inside. Ann flung open the door of the east room, where she and her husband slept. It was a small room, and the big iron bedstead almost filled it. There was a truckle bed, too, for Michael — a small, low bed which was pushed under the big bed when it was not in use. It was pulled out now, and the covers were pushed back, but Michael was not there. The room was empty .

'Oh, my God,' cried Ann. 'Where is he?'

Bess set up a renewed barking, and suddenly Caitriona understood. She ran outside, and Bess ran too, speeding across the yard, just glancing over her shoulder to see whether Caitriona was still following her. Through the cabbage garden she went, and out into the Togher Field.

There, at the back of the *cathair*, the ancient fort, was a drinking place for the cattle. Over the years it had become muddied and foul from the cattle's heavy trampling, and during the winter Tom had wired it off. But one of the cattle must have damaged the wire: there was a gap in it, and there, at the edge of the drinking place, his petticoat caught by a piece of broken wire, was Michael. He was not crying, to Caitriona's amazement; but as she came nearer, she could see that the poor little boy was being violently sick.

As soon as he saw her, Michael gave one more

choke and spewed out the last remains of the filthy water. He held up his arms to Caitriona; she picked him up and hugged him, while Bess stood on her hind legs and licked his dirty face.

'Da, Ma!' shrieked Caitriona, looking at Michael's white face with alarm. It was not like him to be silent. A moment later, however, when his mother and father came running through the orchard, Michael recovered enough to let out a mighty yell.

'Oh, Michael, what happened to you?' cried his mother, taking her baby from Caitriona's arms.

'Me falled in nasty mud,' gulped Michael. 'Bess pull me, an' then she wun away an' get Mammy.'

'Don't worry about it now, Ann,' said Tom. 'Better get him back inside and get him washed. It's a good job he got sick. That water might have poisoned him otherwise.'

As Ann carried Michael back towards the house, Tom stood for a moment looking at the cattle drinking spot and the muddy footprints around it.

'Do you know what, Caitriona?' he said. 'I think Michael slipped in the mud, and his petticoat caught on the wire and he couldn't get himself out. He started to yell, and Bess heard him and came running. You know what she's like; she's always minding him. She pulled him out of the water. He must have fallen into it by that stage, probably face-down. He would have drowned if she hadn't got him out. The mud is so thick he couldn't have freed himself, and ...'

Suddenly he broke off and picked Bess up in his arms, hugging her and hiding his face in her glossy

black fur. Caitriona could see Bess trying to lick his cheeks, and she knew that her father was crying. She started to cry too, and that made Tom give a watery smile.

'We're a fine pair, aren't we,' he said, with an attempt at a laugh. 'We should be singing for joy, instead of crying.'

Caitriona could not stop crying, now she had started. The thought of her darling little brother drowning in the muddy water made her tears come faster and faster, chasing each other down her cheeks.

'Here,' said her father, 'you take Bess. She'll cheer you up. I'll sit here on the stone and you sit on my lap, and Bess can sit on your lap. Isn't she the wonderful dog? She should have a medal.'

After that Caitriona had to stop crying; she started to laugh instead. Then she and her father went over the whole story again, wondering how Bess could possibly have heard Michael, up in the Togher Field, from away down beside the river.

'Let's say a little prayer at the shrine of St Brigid,' said Tom eventually. 'We'll say thank you for sparing Michael's life.'

On the eastern side of the *cathair* there was a wedge-shaped stone shrine. It was quite small, its walls rough and uneven and its slanting roof encrusted with lichen. Inside it was a small stone statue of a woman. Together they knelt there and prayed for a few minutes. Bess sat beside Caitriona, looking serious.

'Let's go back inside,' said Caitriona, when they rose to their feet. 'I want to see Michael and make sure he's all right.'

By the time they got back in, Michael was out of his bath. Wrapped in a big towel, he was sitting on his mother's knee, playing with his toes. Caitriona could not stop kissing him. He looked so sweet, with his blond hair curling over his head and his fat little face smiling once more.

'Well, we're going to have to have a fine celebration tonight,' said Tom, taking the little boy on his knee. 'What about the fish, Caitriona? Did you catch any?'

'Oh, I forgot about the fish,' said Caitriona joyfully. 'Bess and I will go down and get them. I have one for everyone.'

'And me?' said Michael.

'And you,' said Caitriona, kissing him again.

'And Bess?' enquired Michael.

Tom laughed. 'You're right, son,' he said. 'If it weren't for Bess you wouldn't be here now. Take all the time you like, Caitriona; your Ma still has to boil the potatoes and get the fire going.'

Ann got to her feet, hesitated and then went over to the open door where Bess was standing, looking hopefully in, her fringed tail wagging with happiness. She looked slightly alarmed when Ann approached; she had learned to be very wary of her. But this time Ann did not shoo her away. Instead, she bent down and stroked Bess gently. Caitriona and her father exchanged smiles. From now on, they knew, Bess would be a member of the household.

# CHAPTER THREE

It was just as well that Bess's place in the household was secure, because a couple of months later disaster struck. July was always a difficult month. The main food for most families was the potato; it was cheap to grow, and every family grew enough to last them through the winter. However, by June or July, last summer's potatoes had all been used, and the new ones would not be ready until the end of August. These were the hungry months for some families; even for the slightly better off, such as the McMahons, it was a time when any spare savings had to be used to buy expensive wheat flour so that soda bread could take the place of potatoes.

And it was at the end of July that the bailiff arrived.

He was a small, squat, insignificant man, and when he arrived on horseback at the avenue gates, Caitriona was amazed to see her father hurriedly drop his shovel and run to open the gates so that the man would not have to dismount. She wondered whether to follow, but decided not to. She would take Bess, she decided, and walk her among the sheep. She was doing this every day, so that Bess would get used to the sheep and not get excited by them. Tom thought they could start training Bess properly any day; all the lambs were getting quite big, so their mothers were not as protective of them any more.

Caitriona stayed in the Rough Field until she saw the bailiff ride down the avenue. Then she went slowly back towards the house. Her father had not come out yet. That was a bad sign.

The door was standing open, and she could hear her stepmother's sharp voice as she crossed the yard.

'And there's that dog to feed as well!' she was saying.

'She doesn't take much,' said Tom soothingly.

'It's more than we can afford,' replied his wife bitterly.

There was a silence; then Tom said quietly, 'I'm only thankful we had her, or else we wouldn't have Michael any more.'

'That's true,' Ann replied softly, and when Caitriona pushed open the door she could see that her stepmother's eyes were full of tears.

'What's wrong?' she asked. 'What's happened?'

'It's nothing to concern you, love,' said Ann. 'We're just a bit worried, that's all.'

'Well, tell me,' said Caitriona. 'I'm not a child. Tell me what's wrong. Don't leave me going around trying to guess.'

'It's the bailiff,' said her father quietly. 'It seems we owe a bit of rent that we didn't know about. It's just that it's come at a bad time.'

'But how could you not know about it? You always pay him, at each quarter.'

'Well, to be honest, that's just his way of putting it. They've put up the rent on me again. They think they can keep squeezing more and more out of me.'

Caitriona's face was white with shock. 'But they can't do that. It's not fair!'

'Life's not fair,' said Tom. 'It's certainly not fair for us poor folk. We have to pay for this and pay for that — pay dues to Protestant clergy, even though we never darken the doors of their church from one end of the year to the other .... It's no wonder that people like those Whiteboys are out at night, burning and shooting.'

Ann shot him a warning glance. 'That's dangerous talk,' she said. 'No one ever got anywhere with talk like that.'

'Well, perhaps someday they will, please God. Perhaps someday Ireland will be free.'

Caitriona was silent. She knew that her step-mother was right: this was dangerous talk. Only a week before, a man in Ennistymon, only seven miles from Drumshee, had been burned to death in his house by English soldiers. There were rumours everywhere that French ships and French soldiers were going to arrive at any moment, and that they would fight to free Ireland from the English.

In the meantime, it was important to tread carefully. Caitriona knew that her father would have to pay the extra rent that had been demanded; if he did not, their house and farm would be taken from them.

'What about going fishing?' she said suddenly.

Tom and Ann stared at her.

'What in God's name are you talking about?' said Tom impatiently. 'If you want to go fishing, go fishing, but let me have a bit of peace while I try to figure out what to do.'

'No, you don't understand,' said Caitriona. 'I meant why not go sea-fishing and sell the fish afterwards? Do you remember when we went with Uncle

Ned and we caught all that mackerel? We had so many that we smoked them and they lasted all winter. You know Uncle Ned said you could borrow the boat whenever you wanted it, because his rheumatics are too bad now for him to go out.'

Tom's eyes met his wife's.

'It's an idea,' Ann said thoughtfully. 'I can manage here. There's nothing much to be done at the moment. Joe O'Donoghue will give me a hand if ever I need it.'

'I don't think I could manage on my own in the boat, though,' Tom said. 'You really need one person at the oars and one to fish. It was a good idea, Caitriona, but I can't think of anyone to come with me — and even if I did, we'd have to share the profits, and that might not be worthwhile.'

Caitriona took a long breath. Here comes the difficult bit, she thought.

'You could take me,' she said, in a voice which shook slightly, although she tried to make it casual.

'Nonsense!' Ann said sharply; but out of the corner of her eye, Caitriona could see that her father was at least turning over the idea. He knew she was good at fishing; and she had been out in the boat with him and Uncle Ned last summer, when she was a year younger and a year smaller, and he knew that she could row well enough to hold the boat steady while he fished.

'Please,' she said. 'I know I could do it. You said how useful I was last summer. You know you can't manage by yourself.'

'I don't know what to say,' said her father slowly. 'I know you can do it — you're great at fishing — but

29

I don't know that it's girls' work.'

'Better than being thrown out of our house and home,' said Caitriona quickly.

'And there's your Ma,' Tom went on. 'How is she going to manage without either of us?'

Caitriona's heart began to thump. She was going to win, she knew it. Her stepmother was always saying how useless Caitriona was; she would never admit to being unable to do without her.

She was right. Ann looked outraged.

'I can manage,' she said tartly. 'I don't think it's suitable for a girl of twelve to go off fishing. It's bad enough the way she runs around here with her skirt nearly up to her knees. But she's your daughter. It's up to you.'

'Well,' said Tom, considering, 'there's no denying that it's a good idea, and it might just tide us over until the potatoes come through. He's given me a month to find that extra rent, and that should be plenty of time: we'll go out tomorrow and come back in time for the market at Ennis. I'm a bit worried about leaving you alone, Ann, but the O'Donoghues will always lend a hand if you need anything. And you have Bess, too.'

'Oh, can't we take Bess?' said Caitriona, horrified at the idea of being without her dog for days.

'Have some sense,' said her father, shortly. 'What would we do with a dog on the boat? We'll have little enough room for the fish as it is.'

Caitriona said no more. He was right, of course, and it was only for a few days; but she did wish that she could bring Bess. Bess would really enjoy the sea. In spite of her early experience of being half-drowned in the river, she loved swimming, and every morning Caitriona gave her a swim in the pool in the river.

'I'll be back by Saturday, at the latest,' she promised Bess. 'You stay here like a good dog and mind Michael.'

Bess wagged her tail, as if she understood. But the next morning, as Tom and Caitriona set off for the little fishing village of Liscannor, Bess kept following the cart. In the end, Caitriona was forced to lock her in the cabin. She hated to do it, and she hated to hear Bess crying as she ran back down the avenue, but she knew that her father was getting impatient. The sun was beginning to rise, and the sooner they could start their fishing the better.

For a while Caitriona felt very sad and lonely at the thought of Bess crying alone in the cabin; but as they came nearer to the sea, and she heard the seagulls shrieking and tasted the salt on her lips, she began to get excited. When they came to Ned's cottage she jumped down and ran in happily. She was very fond of her Uncle Ned — although he was not really her uncle at all, as he was Ann's brother. He was very good-natured, and although he was in constant pain from his rheumatism, he always had a smile and a joke for Caitriona.

'Well, that's great,' he said, when he heard that she was to go out fishing with her father. 'She'll be fine, Tom. She's a great hand with the boat and a great swimmer. She'll need something a bit warmer than that dress, though. It doesn't look as if there's much wear left in that, and it's cold out there on the Atlantic.'

'What about young Ned's old jerkin and breeches?' said his wife tentatively. 'You can pretend she's a boy. I'll give her a woollen cap and she can push her hair under it. It would probably be best; there's a lot of rough men out fishing these days, and you don't want to call attention to her.'

Tom started to laugh. 'I don't know what her Ma would say to that,' he said. 'But it's not a bad idea. She'll be nice and warm.'

Caitriona quickly skipped off with her aunt before he could change his mind.

'Boys' clothes are really nice and warm and comfortable, aren't they?' she said after she had changed her clothes. 'Boys have much more luck than girls.'

'Ah, wait until you're a bit older,' smiled her aunt. 'Then you'll enjoy wearing pretty clothes. Come on, let's go back and show you to the men.'

'She makes a great boy,' said Uncle Ned when she came in. 'You'll have to call her Ciaran now,' he added, enjoying the joke.

'Don't you ever tell your mother on me,' said Tom warningly.

'No, I won't, I promise,' giggled Caitriona.

Tom picked up the oars. 'Well,' he said, 'let's make a start. The boat's in the usual place, Ned, is it?'

'In the usual,' replied Ned. 'Just beside the harbour. It's turned over, but sure, there'll always be a few idlers standing around who'll lend you a hand to get it on the water.'

Uncle Ned's boat was a currach, a small boat made from cowhide stretched over a wooden frame and heavily painted with tar. It was quite light; Tom and another man easily tipped it over on its side and, carrying it on their heads and shoulders, walked down the strand and launched it on the sea. Caitriona was already standing in the water, ready to steady the currach.

'In you go,' said Tom, and Caitriona was over the side in a flash. It was wonderful to be wearing breeches rather than an awkward, enveloping skirt.

'Dig the oar into the sand to hold it steady while I get in,' said her father, handing her a wooden oar.

That was a bit more difficult. Caitriona was not quite strong enough to hold the boat steady; it spun around and around, until the man who had helped carry the currach came to the rescue.

'You haven't grown enough muscle yet,' he said with a friendly grin.

Caitriona blushed, but said nothing. She was afraid that he might know from her voice that she was a girl.

It was a lovely day, and soon the fish started biting. Tom had brought a net which they could hang over the side of the boat, so any fish they caught could stay nice and cool in that all day long. Soon the net was full, almost to breaking point, and the boat began to lurch ominously to one side. Caitriona and her father shifted their weight to the other side as best they could, but the boat still dipped a little, and water began to come in.

'Better get rid of that quickly, Caitriona,' grunted Tom. 'Use that old pot there — scoop out as much water as you can. I'll lean back as far as I can, to balance your weight while you're doing it. I think we'll make for the shore. We can try selling this lot now, and then we'll bring out two nets with us tomorrow. Who would have thought we'd do so well? We've only been out for a couple of hours.'

Caitriona, baling out the water, glanced up. What she saw made her stop, the pot held in one hand, rigid with fear. There, between them and the Aran Islands, was a huge ship. Obviously no one on board had seen the tiny currach, low down in the water. The ship was bearing down on them at what seemed like a terrifying speed.

# CHAPTER FOUR

Although everything must have happened within moments, it seemed to Caitriona, afterwards, that it had all occurred in slow motion. First the currach began to spin, as it was caught in the trough of a wave; then it tilted; and then Caitriona was flung out, and the ice-cold water closed over her head. With complete clarity, to the end of her days, she remembered how she struggled to free herself of the terrible weight of water which engulfed her.

As she burst through to the surface of the water, her first thought was one of thankfulness that she was not wearing a dress to drag around her legs. Her next thought was to look around for her father. She could not see him, but it was hard to see anything with the sea tossing and bubbling around her. She concentrated on kicking as hard as she could, lifting her arms and curving them to cut through the water. Her woollen hat fell off and she felt her wet hair tumble down over her shoulders.

It was then that she heard a shout from the great ship, which was still ominously close to her. She did not know what the words meant; they were in a strange language. Caitriona knew English, but this was definitely not English. Many months later, Serge told her what he had said and made her repeat the words after him: 'Sacrebleu! C'est une jeune fille!'

Now, however, she was only conscious that help was coming. A young man, dressed in a blue jacket and white breeches, had dived off the forecastle of the ship and was swimming towards her. Caitriona waited, treading water to keep herself afloat, while he came nearer and nearer, swimming so powerfully that he seemed to cover the distance as fast as any boat.

'Do not struggle,' he said in very good English, but with a strange accent.

'My father — can you see him?' gasped Caitriona.

'Do not worry about your father; he will be rescued. He is holding to the oar. It is well with him.'

At that moment, another man dived from the top of the ship. Caitriona could see her father; he was indeed holding on to an oar. But there seemed to be no sign of Uncle Ned's boat.

'I can swim,' she said indignantly to her rescuer.

'Do not struggle,' he said again. Caitriona resigned herself to being towed along like a dead fish.

There was a lot of shouting from on board the ship, still in that strange language which she could not understand, and then a rope ladder was lowered and Caitriona's rescuer seized it with his free hand.

'You can climb?' he asked.

'Yes,' she said. Holding on tightly, she climbed up. Her knees felt weak, but she climbed as quickly as she could, driven by her anxiety to see if her father was all right.

As soon as she reached the top, she could see Tom in the water. Another man — much older than her rescuer, but wearing the same uniform — was swimming beside him. Her father, Caitriona was glad to see, was swimming quite strongly, so he must be uninjured.

Soon he reached the rope ladder; and then he dived down into the water and came up, with a shout of triumph, holding the edge of Uncle Ned's boat. The fragile currach had a nasty hole in its side, but otherwise it was undamaged. Not only that, but the net full of fish was, by some miracle, still attached to the boat.

There was a great cheer of '*Bravo!*' from the deck. One of the men flung down a rope, and Tom, holding on to the end of the rope ladder with one hand, tied the end of the rope securely to the currach with his other hand. He tipped the net of fish into the currach; then, letting the little boat float on the sea behind the big ship, he climbed nimbly on board and hugged Caitriona.

'You all right, love?' he asked. 'Not hurt?'

Caitriona shook her head. Now that it was all over, she did not quite know whether to laugh or cry. But it was all rather exciting — the huge ship, and all the dashing young men in their colourful clothes — and she and her father were all right, and Uncle Ned's boat would be easily mended; so all in all, she decided to laugh. She shook her heavy brown hair off her face, threw back her head and laughed and laughed. The sailors laughed too, and the seagulls overhead shrieked with merriment.

'*Bravo, Mademoiselle!*' said the young man who had rescued her. '*Vous êtes très brave.*'

That must mean brave, thought Caitriona.

'*Elle est jolie, la petite,*' said another man.

That must mean jolly, thought Caitriona, but her rescuer translated:

'He means that you are very pretty.'

Caitriona blushed. For a while now, she had been beginning to think that she might be rather pretty. Her stepmother had an old looking-glass, and from time to time Caitriona peeped in it. She thought her hair was rather nice; it was brownish-black, very long and very shiny. She liked her eyes, too — she thought they were a nice dark blue — but she often wished that she had pinker cheeks. People were always telling her that she looked pale.

Tom, however, was taking no notice of the compliments paid to his daughter.

'Oh, Lord,' he murmured. 'It's the French!'

And suddenly Caitriona understood. For the past six months there had been talk about the French coming. They had landed at Bantry Bay, people said, and there had been terrible trouble. They had come to free the Irish from the rule of England, but that had not happened yet: just terrible things like that man in Ennistymon, only two miles from Liscannor Bay, who had been set alight and burned to death in his own house.

The captain of the ship spoke to the young man who had rescued Caitriona. He listened intently and then turned to Tom McMahon.

'Monsieur,' he said with a little bow, which Caitriona thought was most elegant. 'My captain asks your pardon for the damage to your boat. He will pay you some money, some gold for it. He asks also if he can buy your beautiful fish. They will make a good supper for us all.'

'Well,' said Tom, speaking slowly and carefully, 'tell your captain that he is welcome to the fish. I would give them to him, except that I am a very poor man and I need money for my rent. Please ask him if he can put us ashore at Liscannor.'

There was a rapid conversation between the two men; Caitriona could see the captain shaking his head, so she was not surprised when the young man said: 'My captain is very sorry. He cannot put you on the shore here. Too many soldiers. He will put you on the shore in a more empty place, perhaps Mayo.'

'Mayo!' said Tom, aghast. 'We can't go to Mayo. How could we get home? That's half the country away.'

'He is very sorry,' repeated the young man, with an anxious expression.

It's a shame, thought Caitriona. A minute ago, everyone was laughing and cheering, and now everything's being spoilt.

'Ask him how much gold,' she urged her father in a whisper. 'It might be enough to take us back from Mayo and pay the rent as well. Ask him.'

Obviously the young man understood English better than he spoke it, because again there was a quick conversation between him and the captain. Then he turned back to Tom.

'How much for your rent?' he asked.

'Five pounds.'

I thought it was three, thought Caitriona, but she said nothing.

'We give you ten pounds,' said the captain, and he held up his ten fingers to show them.

Ten pounds! Caitriona caught her breath and looked at her father. Ten pounds could mean the end of all his worries.

Tom, however, was a noted bargainer. He held up his ten fingers and then two more.

'Twelve,' he said. 'I'll have to make a new boat. I'll never get that back from Mayo.'

The captain laughed and nodded. They shook hands, and everyone laughed again.

'What is your name, Mademoiselle?' asked the young man.

'Caitriona.'

'I am named Serge Dupont, at your service.' Again he made a very elegant bow. 'Come, I will show you both your cabin and find you some dry cloths.'

Clothes, I suppose he means, thought Caitriona. Unlike most of the Irish people at that time, both she and her father spoke good English. Tom had an aunt who lived in England; he had been brought up by her, and had only come back to Ireland when he was fourteen years old.

'You had better find some dry clothes for yourself, Serge,' she said shyly. 'You'll catch cold if you don't.'

'Soldiers do not catch cold,' he said, laughing. '*Regardez* — I mean, look — it is your fish.'

Already the net of fish was being hauled into the ship. It should make a good supper, even for all these men, thought Caitriona as she and her father followed Serge.

The room he showed them into was tiny. It made Caitriona's little room in the loft of the cottage at Drumshee seem like a palace.

Tom looked around dubiously. 'I think I'll leave this place to you,' he said. 'I'll spend the night on deck. I'd feel like a rat in a trap in here.'

'It'll be useful for changing,' said Caitriona, 'but I think I'll go on deck too. I'd love to be out at sea in the night.'

Serge was some time in coming back; he was evidently having some trouble in finding the right size of clothes for Caitriona. But the ones that he brought satisfied her. There were a pair of white breeches — too big, but with a belt to hold them in place — and a knitted jersey, with a fine blue coat to go over it all. Tom went off with Serge to get some clothes for himself, leaving her to change. By the time she came back on deck, he was warming himself by teaching the French sailors how to do an Irish dance.

Serge was still in his wet clothes, Caitriona noticed, but she was too shy to say anything more about them. He bowed to her.

'You will dance with me, Mademoiselle Caitriona?' he said, pronouncing her name in a very strange way.

Caitriona began to feel quite excited, quite reckless.

'Don't stand on my feet,' she warned.

'You have lost your shoes in the water?'

'Oh, no,' explained Caitriona, 'I never wear shoes. Shoes cost too much money.'

'You are very poor, then,' he said sympathetically. 'That is why we French have come to rescue you poor Irish from the English. The great general, Napoleon, he have sent us. But we will not talk, but dance! First I will take off my boots, so that I do not hurt you, and then you will show me the Irish dancing. Perhaps you will teach me some Irish words and I will teach you some French ones.'

'You hum for us, Da,' said Caitriona.

'It's a pity I didn't bring my pipe,' said her father. 'I would have, if I'd known the company we were going to meet.'

'He is a very funny man, your father,' said Serge as they danced. 'He always makes jokes, no?'

'Yes,' said Caitriona. That sounded so silly that she started to giggle again. What would her step-mother say if she could see her dancing with a French soldier on board a French ship? That thought made her giggle even more. Soon she was laughing so hard that she had to stop dancing and lean against the rail of the ship.

'Ouf!' said Serge. He stopped too and stood beside her, his clothes steaming in the warm sunshine. 'Your Irish dancing is very fast, no?'

'Yes,' said Caitriona again, and battled with her-self to stop giggling. She must sound so silly to this handsome young Frenchman!

'Sing a song for him, Caitriona,' commanded Tom. 'Sing that song I taught you a while back — that one I learned at the fair.'

And so, while her father hummed the tune, Caitriona lifted her voice and sang the song. She tried to sing it as well as she could, as well as she had sung it that night for old Mr Quin, and to remember everything she had been taught. She listened critically as she sang, and even to herself it sounded good.

However, she wasn't prepared for what came next. All of the men on the deck stopped working and gathered around her; even the men on the rig-ging had stopped climbing. The whole ship was listening. Bravely Caitriona went on with the song, letting her voice soar to its highest notes, and when she had finished everyone clapped their hands and shouted *Bravo!*

'Aren't Frenchmen nice?' said Caitriona in a low

voice to her father. 'They're much nicer than Irishmen.'

'Now I will sing you a French song,' said Serge. 'I am not as good a singer as Mademoiselle, although my mother, who is a teacher of singing, has done her best to teach me.'

He's a good singer, thought Caitriona, listening carefully. He had a light voice, but a very tuneful one. She did not understand the song, but she was determined to learn it from him sometime. When he had finished she clapped loudly and smiled at him, but by now the other men had drifted away, so he did not get the same applause she had.

Later on, when all the men not on duty had gone below, Caitriona curled up on a pile of blankets on the deck, sleepily listening to her father and Serge talking together. The name of Wolfe Tone was mentioned again and again. Caitriona had heard of Wolfe Tone. He was the one who was organising the United Irishmen. Her father thought he might end up freeing Ireland, but her stepmother thought he was a dangerous man. She's got no courage, thought Caitriona disgustedly. She'll never take a risk about anything. Why did my Da marry her?

For a while, her thoughts drifted away. She was beginning to feel quite sleepy. When she started to listen again, Serge was telling her father about Napoleon Bonaparte, the general of the French army, whom they called 'the Little Colonel'.

'We, we have had our Revolution ten years ago and now we have a glorious country. People have their own land, not just one nobleman owning thousands of acres. Everyone has schooling. For everyone, great or small, there is Liberty, Equality and Fraternity. You too, you in Ireland, will have your revolution, and then you will be a great country also,' he was saying.

Caitriona fell asleep at that stage. She started up, suddenly wide awake, to hear her father saying:

'What is it, lad? Are you sick or something?'

Serge did not reply. He had gone a chalky white, and he was shivering so violently that his teeth were chattering. Tom reached out and put a hand on his forehead.

'He's burning with fever,' he said to Caitriona. Turning to the helmsman, he said urgently: 'Have you got a doctor on this ship?'

The man shook his head, uncomprehending.

'A doctor,' repeated Tom urgently.

This time the man understood. 'No,' he said. 'No doctor.' He looked at Serge indifferently, shrugged his shoulders and turned back to watching the sea.

'We'd better get him to bed, Caitriona,' said Tom. 'We'll take him down to that little cabin he gave you. I think it's probably his. You bring some blankets.'

'I knew he'd catch cold if he didn't change his clothes,' said Caitriona in a frightened whisper, gathering up the blankets, while her father easily lifted the slight young man in his powerful arms and carried him down the steps. They put him on the narrow wooden bunk and covered him with blankets. He was moaning, and his breath was coming in quick short pants.

'How could he get so sick so suddenly, Da? He was all right a little while ago.'

'I think he probably has pneumonia. I remember my mother getting that, and it was just like this. One minute she was as right as rain, and then she was sick; and she just got sicker and sicker, until she died. That was when I got sent to England.'

Caitriona looked at the young man, in his gallant uniform, with horror. Was it possible that he could die?

'I'm going to get the captain,' said her father. 'There's some water in that cask. See if you can get him to drink some.'

In a moment he was gone, and Caitriona was left alone with Serge. She put the water to his lips; he swallowed some, and then sat up in bed with his hand over his mouth. Quick as a flash, Caitriona fetched a basin. She was used to this; Michael had spent much of his first year of life getting sick. Serge was indeed very sick, but, unlike Michael, he did not seem any better after he had vomited. He lay back, groaning.

'Have you a pain?' Caitriona asked softly, bending over him.

He stared at her, his dark brown eyes uncomprehending and almost unfocused. She wished she could speak French. It seemed to be too much of an effort, now, for Serge to talk English.

'Pain?' she said again, and this time he nodded.

'Yes, here.' He pointed to his ribs. 'Very terrible.'

Caitriona wished she could do something to ease his pain — after all, he had saved her life, earlier that day — but she could think of nothing to do. When Michael had a pain in his stomach, Ann heated a stone in the fire and wrapped it in cloths to lay against the pain, but Caitriona could not think how to do that on board the ship.

'Oh, hurry up, Da,' she said under her breath.

# CHAPTER FIVE

For the next few days, Caitriona hardly stirred from the dark, stifling little cabin. Serge was desperately ill, so ill that at times both Caitriona and her father thought he would die. Caitriona felt helpless. There was so little that she could do for him. There was no doctor on the ship, although they did have a medicine chest and she was able to give Serge some laudanum to ease his pain. Day after day she sat by his bed, listening to his rapid breathing and watching his pain-filled eyes, until she almost gave up hope that he would recover.

He's such a nice-looking young man, too, she thought, the tears beginning to run down her cheeks. He has such nice brown eyes and such long eyelashes, and he's been so kind and friendly to me .... With a great effort, she managed to control her sobs. She was overtired, she knew. She must get some sleep, or she would be no use as a nurse.

Caitriona was so tired that she slept for hours; she might have slept for a day, but she was woken up by the realisation that the swaying motion of the ship had ceased. She opened her eyes and looked at Serge.

To her great joy, his eyes were clear; it was obvious that the fever had left him. His breathing, too, was better: he still breathed with a certain amount of caution, but the breaths were definitely deeper and stronger. She bent over him.

'How are you?' she asked gently.

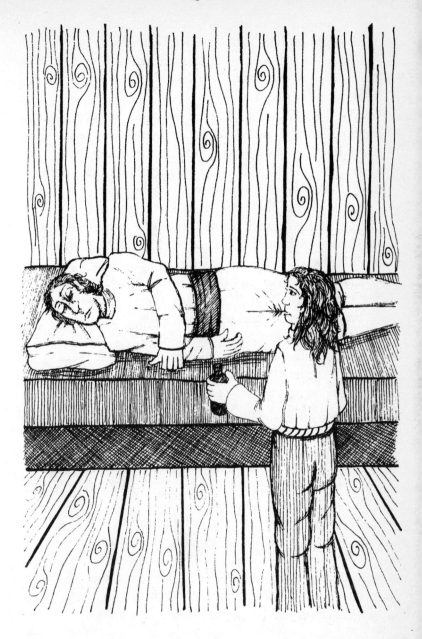

He looked puzzled for a moment, almost as if he had forgotten her. Then his face cleared.

'Ah, Mademoiselle Caitriona,' he said, with a return of his old playful manner. 'You have been looking after me, no?'

'Yes,' said Caitriona, so overjoyed at seeing him better that she began to giggle again, just as if she were back on deck teasing him about his English.

Serge smiled. He was evidently much better, though still very pale and weak-looking.

'Would you like a drink?' asked Caitriona.

He nodded, and drank gratefully when she put the mug to his lips, but he did it slightly absent-mindedly, as if he were listening.

'The ship has stopped,' he said suddenly. 'We have arrived. The fighting commences. I must get up. Where are my *vêtements* — my cloths?'

He made a great effort and sat up, but had to lie back again from sheer weakness.

'You must stay there,' said Caitriona severely. 'You've been very sick. You can't get up and fight.'

She spoke as confidently as she could, but she hoped that her father would come soon and make Serge stay in bed.

'Who do you want to fight, anyway?' she asked hurriedly, hoping that if she kept him talking he would forget about getting up.

His eyes widened. 'Your enemies, of course — the English. The ones that keep all you Irish as slaves.'

'Oh,' said Caitriona, rather surprised. She had never thought of herself as a slave. St Patrick had been a slave, but she had never heard of any other slaves in Ireland.

'You hate the English, *n'est-ce pas*?' Serge said eagerly. 'And you hope your country will be freed by the Croppy Boys?'

'I suppose so,' Caitriona said doubtfully. She did not like to tell him that her stepmother always said that people should mind their own business and keep their heads down and stay away from the Whiteboys. She supposed that these Croppy Boys were some kind of Whiteboys.

But it was rather exciting, having all these dashing young Frenchmen coming to free Ireland — as long as nothing happened to them, of course. She looked with alarm at Serge. He seemed determined to get up; he was making feeble efforts to pull himself upright .

At that moment, to Caitriona's relief, the door opened and her father came in, accompanied by the captain. They were both looking rather worried, but at the sight of Serge awake and sitting up the captain's face lightened. He spoke rapidly in French and Serge replied, his voice, though weak, seeming to gain strength from the excitement.

After a few minutes, the captain smiled at Caitriona and went out. Serge started, laboriously, to find the words to tell the McMahons what was happening.

'We go on shore. We are in Killala Bay, in Mayo,' he said. 'We go to fight your enemies, the English. You will come with us. The captain will give you money, and you will find a cart and go back to your home.'

'Good,' said Tom, looking very relieved. Caitriona was not so sure. She would have enjoyed the excitement of a battle, she felt.

'I must say to you, thank you a million times; to you, Monsieur McMahon, and to my little friend Caitriona,' went on Serge. 'The captain, he tell me that you have looked after me all the time and I owe my life to you.'

'That's all right, lad,' said Tom easily, while Caitriona blushed with excitement and embarrassment.

At that moment, one of the men came back, murmured something to Serge in French, and then went out. Serge sighed and sank back on the bed, looking disappointed.

'The captain, he say I am not to fight, for a little while,' he said. 'I am to stay in an inn for a few days with you, and then I will join my companions. While we stay there you can buy your horse and cart and prepare for the journey.'

That night, under cover of darkness, the troops from the French ship disembarked. The French marched for Killala, and Tom, Caitriona and Serge went to stay at an inn.

All day they stayed there, waiting apprehensively for news. Towards nightfall one of the French soldiers came in, full of excitement. Everything was going very well: the French had quickly captured the castle at Killala, and were using it as their headquarters. Hundreds of Irish had joined the French and had been fitted out with uniforms. Victory seemed certain.

The next day, however, Tom went out to buy a cart and came back with a glint of amusement in his eye. Privately, to Caitriona, he whispered that a lot of the people who had joined the French seemed to be doing it for the sake of the fine clothes which they were given, and most of all for the sake of the gun which was issued to each of them.

'You can hear the noise of the shots blasting the crows from one end of the farms to the other,' finished Tom. 'They'll be lucky if they get half the men they've put into uniform to fight for them. Sure, most of the poor fellows here don't know what the whole thing is about. I didn't know very much myself until I had a talk with Serge. I think they know more about it all in Dublin and up in the north. Anyway, I've bought a fine cart and a horse; when they're all safely on their way to Castlebar, we'll make our way home. The lad will be all right here until his friends come back to collect him.'

The next day, however, Serge was in a high fever again. He tossed and turned, muttering in delirium and coughing harshly.

'We can't leave him,' said Tom, looking at him in concern. 'There's no one in the house to nurse him; the man that owns it has gone off to Castlebar with the French, and his wife has gone to stay with her mother. We'll just have to stay with him until he's better, or until the army comes back to their ship.'

For the whole of another anxious week, Caitriona and her father nursed Serge. Luckily the pain did not come back, so he did not have another bout of pneumonia, but there was no doubt that the excitement had brought back the fever and the cough. He was ill, but not very ill, and after a few days Caitriona began to tire of being shut up in one dark room. She longed to go outside.

'Let me buy the bread today,' she begged her father.

'Well, take care. Say as little as possible, but listen all you can. I'd like to hear what's happening.'

Caitriona did not need to do much listening when she went out. The whole town was lit up with excitement. The French and the Irish had attacked the English garrison at Castlebar, and the English had run away!

'Sure, it was as good as the races,' called one wit to another across the street. 'They say the English were so frightened that they never stopped running until they reached Tuam.'

'That's great news,' said Tom, when Caitriona came back. 'Let's hope we go on hearing news like that every day.'

By the end of the week, though, the news was no longer good. No other ships arrived from France; and on 8 September, the tiny army of eight hundred and fifty Frenchmen surrendered to a massive force of ten thousand Englishmen. The French soldiers were taken prisoner and marched across to Dublin.

'There's only one thing to do,' said Tom firmly to the despairing Serge. 'You'll have to come back to Drumshee with us. We can't leave you here; you'd be in jail a few hours after we were gone. You come to Drumshee. We'll keep you there until all the excitement dies down, and then we'll get you back to France, somehow or other.'

# CHAPTER SIX

**I**t was getting dark when they arrived at Drumshee, a week later. Caitriona had never been so glad, in all her life, to see the familiar gates. Quickly she climbed down from the cart and opened them.

After the cart had gone through, Caitriona stood still for a moment and then made up her mind. For some strange reason, she didn't want to be present while her father was telling her stepmother about Serge.

'You go on up, Da,' she said. 'I'm so stiff with the jolting that I don't think I could stand another minute sitting there. I'll walk up the lane and through the Togher Field.'

As Caitriona walked up the shadowy path, it seemed to her that she had been absent from her home for years rather than weeks. It had been dangerous, but it had been more exciting than anything else which had ever happened to her. She wondered whether it would be dull, being back home; but then she thought of Serge and smiled to herself. Life was going to be different from now on.

Halfway up the lane, Caitriona turned in through the ivy-covered posts of the gate to the Togher Field — and then stopped. A small black shadow was coming down the hillside with incredible speed. Before Caitriona could draw breath, Bess had catapulted herself into her arms.

Caitriona hugged her and kissed her, but that was

not enough for Bess. She wriggled and twisted and burrowed her head into Caitriona's neck, almost as if she was trying to get inside her. Her breath came in quick, short pants, her floppy ears were strained back against her head, and her pink tongue was frantically licking every inch of Caitriona's face.

'Oh, Bess,' said Caitriona, almost in tears. 'You're so thin! She hasn't been feeding you properly. I hate her! Oh, Bess, I'll never leave you again. I promise. If I go away again, I'll take you with me.'

Bess almost seemed to understand. Her tail wagged even faster, and when Caitriona put her gently on the ground, Bess ran around and around in circles, playfully pawing the ground and prancing like a little horse.

'Come on,' said Caitriona. 'Let's show you to Serge.'

Suddenly all her weariness vanished and she started to run up the steep Togher Field. Bess ran too, circling around and around Caitriona as if she could not bear to take her eyes off her beloved mistress for even a second.

When they came into the orchard, Caitriona slowed down and stopped. Suddenly, she felt shy and slightly embarrassed. She did not want to go into the cottage straight away. She wondered again what her stepmother would think about her father bringing one of the French home. I'll stay out for a while and give Da a chance to talk her around, she thought.

The orchard was almost dark, the old apple trees casting their immense shadows on the ground. Caitriona bent down and picked up a small apple from the ground. It tasted sharp, slightly bitter, but it was incredibly juicy. She chewed it thoughtfully, leaning against the tree and feeling the warmth of Bess against her legs. She took another large bite of the apple and put the piece in Bess's mouth, smiling to herself when she heard the quick crunch; Bess loved apples, but she never really got value from them, as she swallowed them down so quickly.

'Come on, Bess, come and meet Serge,' she said, tossing her apple core to Bess, who caught it neatly and swallowed it in two seconds.

The sound of voices and of Serge's laugh reassured Caitriona as she crossed the cabbage garden. There was unlikely to be any trouble if he was laughing already. She smiled to herself as she crossed the yard. He probably paid Ma a few compliments, she thought. By now Ann, like Caitriona, would be a slave to Serge's charm.

It was a warm evening, and both halves of the door were standing open. Caitriona peeped in. Serge was sitting on Tom's special chair, beside the fire, with Michael sitting on his knee. Ann was standing by the window, looking white and apprehensive.

Michael was the first one to see Caitriona. He jumped down from Serge's knee and rushed across to her.

'Tatty!' he cried, his fat little arms held up to her. 'Tatty, you tum home!'

Caitriona picked him up and hugged him. Suddenly it was lovely to be home again. She put Michael down gently.

'What a big boy you are,' she said lovingly. 'You're nearly as big as Bess now, Michael.'

'So, and *voilà* Bess,' said Serge. 'Come to me, Bess, you little Irish dog with the name of an English queen.'

Bess took one hesitant step into the kitchen. She looked appealingly at Ann, her tail wagging.

'She is shy, yes?' asked Serge.

'She isn't allowed into the kitchen,' said Caitriona briefly. 'Come outside with me, Serge. She's a very friendly dog. You'll love her.'

'What nonsense,' said Ann. 'Serge mustn't go out in the night air. He'll be getting that pneumonia back again. Let the dog come in for once, Caitriona. Her feet look clean.'

Cautiously, with her head held low, Bess advanced into the kitchen. She circled around and around Serge, her tail wagging and her lips pulled back from her teeth in a grin.

'Bess is smiling!' said Michael with delight.

'Oh, what a lovely dog,' said Serge, bending to fondle the silky ears. He held out his hands; Bess put her two front paws into them, and they both began to circle around the kitchen in an awkward kind of dance, while Michael screamed with laughter.

'You'll need some music for that,' said Tom, and he took down his pipe and began to play a lively jig.

'Me dance, too,' said Michael, holding up his arms, so Caitriona danced with him.

They were all making so much noise that it was a miracle that anything else could be heard above it, but Ann's apprehensive ears caught the rumble of cartwheels on the cobbles in the yard.

'Quick,' she said urgently. 'Caitriona, take Serge into our bedroom. We mustn't let anyone see him.

Stay with him, no matter who it is. We can't risk any gossip about him in the neighbourhood.'

Quickly Caitriona picked up Bess, caught Serge by the hand and dragged him into the east bedroom. As she closed the door behind them, she heard her father starting to play the tune again. Signalling to Serge to sit on the bed, she went to the window and cautiously peeped out.

They had been just in time: Mr and Mrs O'Donoghue's cart was coming around the corner. It could have been worse — it might have been the soldiers — but Caitriona knew that Ann had been right, so she crouched in the shadow of the curtains and put her finger across her lips to warn Serge to keep quiet .

The bedroom door was ancient and ill-fitting, so Caitriona could hear the conversation as well as if she were in the outer room. Despite her worries about Serge, she found it hard not to giggle at the story which her father was spinning, about the boat being washed out to sea and the two of them landing up in Connemara and some kindly folk helping them to get home ....

Serge was smiling at her. She hastily looked away and started to comb Bess's coat with her fingers. Bess had been a bit neglected while they had been away, so Caitriona concentrated on teasing out a knot in the silky hair. She was so busy doing this that she lost some of the conversation, but then she heard her father saying loudly and clearly:

'Don't worry about a thing, Joe. You were very good to help while I was away. Now that I'm back, I can manage it all. In any case, I have one of my cousin's lads coming down from the north for a few weeks. He'll be able to help me with everything. He's a fine young fellow.'

Caitriona put her hand over her mouth to keep in a giggle, but she became serious when she heard Joe O'Donoghue's next words.

'Whose lad would that be, Tom? I didn't know you had a cousin up north. Would that be one of the Carneys, then?'

His voice was slow and casual, with curiosity rather than suspicion in it. Nevertheless, Caitriona bit her lip with anxiety. Her father should have known better. In this part of the world, everyone knew everyone else's relations.

Tom's voice, however, showed no signs of worry.

'That's right, Joe, it's one of the Carneys. I should have said second cousin, rather than cousin. To be honest with you, I'm not too sure what the relationship is, but I'm looking forward to seeing the lad when he arrives. Will you have another drop of the elderberry, Joe? And what about you, Missus? You'll take something?'

Oh, go away, Caitriona screamed in her mind. Desperately she willed Joe O'Donoghue to say that he had to go, that he had to be up early to go to the market, anything to get the two of them out of the house; but no, she could hear the clank of the bottle against the glasses, and she knew they were settling in for a long evening.

'Where's Caitriona, then?' said Joe, after a few noisy gulps. 'Would she come and sing a song for us?'

To her horror, Caitriona heard Michael say, 'She in Mammy bed,' and heard him start to toddle across the floor. She held her breath, but a rustle of skirts told her that Ann had jumped up and seized him.

'The poor child was very tired, Joe, after all their adventures and all the time it took them to come back. '

At that, Tom gave a mighty yawn, and once again Caitriona pressed her knuckles to her mouth to stop herself from laughing.

'Well, you must be tired out too, Tom,' said Joe. Caitriona could hear, from the different sound of his voice, that he had got to his feet. 'We won't be keeping you. When we saw the cart go up the avenue we just thought we'd come over and make sure you were all right.'

'You're a great neighbour, Joe. I don't know how we'd manage without you.'

Yes, Joe, you're great, echoed Caitriona in her mind, but just go home now, like a good man. She looked across at Serge. He had sunk down on Tom and Ann's bed, and looked as if he had fallen asleep. He's still not very strong after the pneumonia, she thought. He probably shouldn't have been dancing around the room like that.

As she looked at Serge, she suddenly thought of the man in Ennistymon who had been covered with boiling oil and set alight. She shuddered. She could not bear anything to happen to Serge. Whatever happened, she had to keep him safe.

The O'Donoghues were going; Caitriona could hear chairs being scraped back on the flagstoned floor. They said good-bye, and the two McMahons said polite meaningless things — 'Do you have to go so early?' and 'Sure the night is still young'. And then, at last, came the noise of cartwheels on the cobbles of the yard; the cart's shadow passed the window, and the cart rumbled on down the avenue.

Serge was fast asleep. Moving cautiously so as not to wake him, Caitriona went to the door and noiselessly lifted the latch.

'Tom,' came her stepmother's sibilant whisper, 'we can't keep that boy here. It's much too dangerous. Turn him out. Let him fend for himself. He's a soldier, after all.'

'I can't do that, Ann. The lad isn't well. In any case, he'd soon get picked up by the English if he was on his own; he can't even speak the language properly. We can't turn him out. Remember, he saved Caitriona's life. She might have drowned without him.'

'Caitriona, Caitriona — that's all you think about! What about Michael? You know what the English will do to us all if we're caught with a Frenchman here!'

'Look, Ann.' Tom's voice was soothing. 'You're tired and upset. You wouldn't really want me to turn that boy over to the English. There's no danger; we'll just keep him hidden for a week or so, while we get a message to his people in France. I promise you, there's no risk to any of us.'

Blazing with anger, Caitriona jerked the door open and came out.

'Where's the lad?' asked Tom, with a warning look in his eye.

'He's gone to sleep,' said Caitriona, choking back

the angry words with a great effort and trying to pretend that she had not overheard the exchange. 'Are we going to pretend he's one of our cousins from the north?'

'Yes,' said her father, with pride. 'I suddenly thought that was a good idea. We'll have to teach him a bit of Irish, but they have a funny kind of Irish up there anyway, so no one will notice anything if he sounds different. You'll have to be the one to teach him, Caitriona. I was thinking that, when he's a bit stronger, I might set the two of you to work clearing the old *cathair*. There's good earth up there; it would make a good potato garden if the rocks were taken out of it. And it's well-hidden, with all the bushes around it; no one will see him up there. '

'How are we going to get a message to his people over in France?' asked Ann.

'Well, I'll wait for a week or two, until all the excitement about the French dies down,' said Tom. 'And then I think I'll go over to Ned and collect the horse, at least — we can always get the old cart later on. I'll find some ship at Liscannor that's going to France, and we'll send a message by that. The lad says his mother will find a way to send his passage money over to him.'

'We'll have to be very careful until he goes,' said Ann, with a look of apprehension in her eyes.

But then Serge came in, yawning and stretching; Ann's expression changed and she began bustling about, getting the settle-bed ready beside the fire, offering him some elderberry wine. There was no doubt about it, Caitriona realised: her stepmother might be worried and frightened, but she was a different person while this handsome young Frenchman was around.

'Come on, Bess,' she said aloud. 'We're going to have great fun tomorrow, but now it's time for you to go to bed. I'll race you to your cabin.'

# CHAPTER SEVEN

For the next week, Caitriona and Serge worked every day on clearing the stones from the *cathair*. It was a strange place, the *cathair*: an ancient, circular field, surrounded by a deep ditch, with a wall of earth and stones all around it. It only measured about a hundred paces from one side of the circle to the other — that was probably why no one had bothered to clear it before — but the ground was well-drained and fertile. The big problem was that there were innumerable heavy stones buried beneath the grasses and the weeds, littering almost every yard of the enclosure; they made it impossible even to graze the cattle in the field.

At the beginning of the week, Serge was only able to shift the smaller and lighter stones, and he had to take frequent rests; but by the end of the week, he was so much stronger that he was able to lift quite large stones and was rarely out of breath. Serge and Caitriona heaved the stones out of the long grass, one by one, and placed them on top of the new wall which they were building near the eastern entrance to the enclosure.

Serge did not make much progress with learning Irish, however. In the end, in despair, Caitriona decided that she would teach him to sing Irish songs so that he could learn Irish words that way. Like herself, Serge had a good ear; when they sang all the old songs which Caitriona's father had taught her, Serge sounded quite Irish. All day long, as they worked, they sang, until Tom declared that being anywhere near the two of them was like going to a concert.

'You know, Caitriona,' said Serge seriously, 'your voice is the best that I have ever heard, and I have heard many young girls going in and out of my mother's singing school. If she you taught — I mean, if she taught you — in a few years' time you would be on the stage in Paris.'

Caitriona caught her lower lip between her teeth in embarrassment. She looked down at Bess, who was beside her as usual; Bess looked up with her soft brown eyes and wagged her tail. Caitriona hugged her, hiding her blushes in the soft silky ears. Her mind was whirling with excitement. She remembered what Mr Quin had said, that night a while ago when she had sung to him. Perhaps it wasn't such an impossible dream after all. Perhaps she might sing on the stage in London or Paris!

Caitriona raised her head and looked at Serge.

'Would it be possible, do you think?' she said. 'Would your mother teach me?'

It was Serge's turn to look embarrassed.

'She would teach you,' he said, rather shame-facedly, 'but you would have to pay. We are quite poor, my mother and I. She gains her living' — makes her living, I suppose he means, thought Caitriona — 'by taking pupils for singing. And you would need money to live, to feed yourself, to clothe yourself.'

'I suppose so,' said Caitriona slowly. She was sorry she had said anything. It had spoilt the day a bit. She had been silly to think that Serge's mother would teach her for free.

'You see,' explained Serge, watching her face anxiously, 'you could not be trained to be a great singer in a few weeks, or even in a few months. It takes years. My father is dead, so my mother has to work. I have two sisters: Aimée is your age, and Michelle is a year younger. I do not earn much money yet, so I cannot help her very much with them.'

'Let's forget it,' said Caitriona briefly. She looked around for something to distract Serge, to change the subject, and pointed to a large stone on the ground.

'That's a funny stone,' she said. 'I wonder why it's that shape.'

Serge examined it carefully.

'Do you know,' he said, 'I have been noticing that there are two kinds of stone here. Some of it is heavy, dark rocks — what your father calls the greenstone — and some of it is light-coloured stone that is much less heavy. And every time I see some of this light stone, I find that it has been cut by a stonemason. Look at this piece — do you see how it is cut in an up-and-down pattern? It looks like the battlements of a castle. Was there ever a castle here?'

'I don't know,' said Caitriona. 'I can't imagine one. Let's go and ask my father. He's just outside, digging out the cattle drinking place. You come too; there's no one around to see you. If we meet anyone, re-member your name is Patrick. Just hang your head and mutter. Pretend to be shy.'

There was no one about, and Tom was only too glad to leave the unpleasant, heavy work of cleaning out the cattle drinking place and examine the stone instead.

'I think you're right, lad,' he said eventually. 'It does look like the battlements on top of a castle. Do you remember, Caitriona? We saw them on our way back from Mayo. These are the spaces where a man could stand with a gun, or with a bow and arrow.'

'And look at this, too,' exclaimed Serge, who was getting excited. 'This is beautiful stone. It is much too good for the walls, Monsieur McMahon. This is a stone — how do you say? — a mullion from one of the windows of a castle. It is certain: there was once a castle here, in your *cathair*.'

Caitriona flushed with excitement. 'Do you think our family was once rich, long ago, Da?'

'I wouldn't know,' said Tom. 'If they were, they didn't leave much of it behind.'

'What is the name of this stone?' asked Serge.

'That's limestone,' said Tom. 'It comes from the Burren, a few miles from here. It's an easy stone to cut and it looks good. But have you noticed that some of the greenstone has been cut into blocks, as well? Not like the limestone — that's a real stonemason's job — but it's been cut. I was thinking that there was probably a house, or perhaps more than one house, up here at some stage. But you're right: that limestone would have been for something fancier. It must have been a castle. No one would go to the trouble of bringing it all these miles just for an ordinary house.'

'I think I will put all these castle stones together over here,' said Serge decisively. 'Caitriona can help me with the smaller ones. Then, when we are finished, we will think of something fine to do with them. Perhaps your wife would like a little flower-garden, Monsieur McMahon? These beautiful stones would make a very good — how do you say? — border.'

Tom laughed. 'We haven't much time for flowers here, lad,' he said good-naturedly. 'But do what you like with them. And go on with the Irish now, Caitriona. It seems to me that his English is getting better and better, but not his Irish, and that's no good: if he's speaking English, the soldiers will spot his French accent straight away.'

'Yes, Da,' said Caitriona absent-mindedly. Her thoughts were busy with the splendid castle which had once stood inside the *cathair*. Anyone who lived in a castle must have been very rich; perhaps she might find a piece of gold they had lost ....

With renewed energy she went to work, carrying pieces of limestone from the centre of the *cathair*, where most of them had been piled, over to a patch of short grass at the side, and trying to see how they might have fitted together. Serge was as excited as Caitriona was, and she thought he was glad to be handling the light limestone, after all the hard work of lugging the heavy pieces of greenstone about.

'I'll teach you a song about going to a fair in County Clare,' she said. 'When you can sing it properly, I'll tell you what it means in English. Then you can say it in Irish to Da at dinnertime.'

By the end of the morning, most of the centre of the enclosure had been cleared of the broken limestone blocks, and the long grass was all trampled down. Serge and Caitriona looked around in satisfaction. Soon this would be a usable field.

Caitriona kicked the flattened grass, just in case

that gold coin lay hidden somewhere, and her toe felt something metal. She picked it up and held it out to Serge.

'*Eh, voilà!*' he said excitedly. 'There is the proof. That is a piece of the window from your castle. That is very *ancien* — how do you say? — ancient.

Look at the little metal diamond-shapes. See, some glass is still in them.'

The tiny pieces of glass were thick and greenish. They could see the remains of the latch which had held the window. Caitriona turned the bit of glass and metal over and over in her hands. Perhaps, hundreds of years ago, a girl her own age had lived in a castle at Drumshee, and had opened this window and looked out across the Togher Field and down towards the Big Meadow ....

'Let's show it to Da,' she began to say; but just then it started to rain. Caitriona and Serge sheltered under the blackthorn hedge. It wasn't much of a shower, and before it had properly finished, the sun came out. It shone through the raindrops; a glorious rainbow spanned the sky, and seemed to touch the earth right in the centre of the *cathair*.

'*Oh là là!*' said Serge, dropping into French. '*C'est un arc-en-ciel. C'est bien magnifique!*'

'Oh, look, look!' cried Caitriona. 'Look where it's pointing — there. Do you know what that means?'

'No, what?' said Serge, with a puzzled look.

Caitriona took a deep breath. 'It means there's a crock of gold buried there.'

'A crock of gold?' said Serge, puzzled.

'That's what the story says,' explained Caitriona. 'There's a crock of gold buried just where the rainbow ends.'

'It is true, no?' said Serge.

'Yes,' said Caitriona, firmly. 'It is true.' A wave of excitement shot through her. Wouldn't it be wonderful if it were! she thought. Perhaps, if she just believed in it hard enough, it might come true —

perhaps, after all, she might find the money to train as a singer ....

'Come on,' she said, tugging at Serge's arm. 'Let's go back for our dinner. After dinner we'll bring up a shovel and dig till we find the crock of gold, and then I can go to France with you, and your mother can train me to be a singer!'

# CHAPTER EIGHT

After dinner, however, Tom produced an old bottle of thick black ink from the little cupboard, set high in the wall beside the huge fireplace, where all sorts of things like salt were kept so that the damp would not spoil them.

'Go and get a feather from one of the geese, Caitriona,' he said. 'I want to make a pen. Serge can write a letter to his mother, and I'll take the horse and go down to Liscannor. I'll ask Ned's advice; I'll be bound he'll find some boat going across to France which will deliver the letter with no questions asked.'

'I will give you the name of my uncle,' said Serge. 'He has a boat at Saint Malo. He is the brother of my mother. He will deliver the letter to her, and perhaps he will come to collect me himself. Often he brings wine to the city of Galway.'

'This means Serge will be going soon,' Caitriona told Bess, as they ran side by side into the orchard, where two fat geese, accompanied by their goslings, kept the grass around the old apple trees nice and short. Caitriona was a bit wary of the geese — the gander was a wicked bird, especially when he and his wife had goslings — so she kept Bess beside her. The gander made a run at them, stretching his neck out and hissing loudly, but Bess gave a quick short bark and eyed him sternly; he turned away in confusion and began cropping the grass again, viciously tearing up great beakfuls of it. Caitriona found a nice clean feather and took it back to the house.

The meal had been cleared off the table and everyone was sitting around it, looking serious. A letter was a big thing. Caitriona could write — her father had taught her, and every Christmas the two of them wrote a few letters to their relations in England — but no one in the house had ever written a letter to France before.

Caitriona delivered the feather, and Tom took out his knife and began to make a pen. Ann stirred up the sludgy ink and added a few drops of water to it.

Caitriona went out and sat on the step, with her arm around Bess, looking down the hill towards the valley where the River Fergus twisted and curved. I bet Ma can't wait to get rid of him, she thought.

She sighed. She didn't want Serge to go. Life had been colourful and exciting since she had met him. Soon she would be thirteen years old; but what was ahead of her? Just more housework, which she hated — either for her stepmother, or else in service in a big house. In four or five years' time, perhaps, she might get married, and then she would just be doing more housework in yet another house.

She lifted one of Bess's long ears and whispered into it: 'Oh, Bess, I want to be a singer. I would like that more than anything else in the world. I'd like to sing to hundreds of people and have them clap and cheer just like those Frenchmen on the boat.'

Bess turned her head and gave Caitriona an understanding lick. She seemed to sense that Caitriona was upset, so she gravely held out her paw and shook hands with her.

Caitriona had to laugh. She gave Bess a kiss on her silky-smooth forehead, and went back inside.

Everything was quiet in the little room. Michael was asleep, and only the noise of the quill scratching over the page broke the silence. Caitriona went over and sat at the table beside Serge. The words on the page were strange to her — he must be writing in French — but she could see her own name halfway down the paper. She blushed a little, wondering what Serge was saying about her to his mother.

'See,' said Serge, pointing to where her name was written, 'I have told my mother that you have the voice of an angel. That will make my sister Aimée jealous. She thinks that she sings very well, but she does not sing as well as you.'

'Good job Caitriona will never meet her, then,' chuckled Tom. 'Never let two jealous women get together, lad. That's the secret of a happy life.' He winked at Serge and got up to harness the horse.

Perhaps I will meet her, thought Caitriona. She waited until her father had gone, with the letter carefully placed inside his hat, and then tugged at Serge's sleeve.

'Let's go back up to the *cathair*,' she said.

'Oh, why don't you take it easy this afternoon,' said Ann to Serge. 'Tom doesn't mind when that job is done. It was just something to keep you occupied and out of sight.'

Caitriona held her breath. She could not wait to dig in the centre of the *cathair*, where the foot of the rainbow had rested, but she knew better than to mention it to her stepmother. She looked anxiously at Serge, and he got to his feet immediately.

'No, I am enjoying myself,' he said to Ann, with one of his polite little bows. 'The exercise and the fresh air are good for me; I must get hungry for your so delicious food, Madame McMahon. It would be very sad if I could not eat it.'

He seems to think she's something wonderful, thought Caitriona, a little jealously. He doesn't know how much she wants to get rid of him. But she forgot about Ann in her excitement as Serge took her father's shovel from the cabin and set off up the hill, towards the *cathair*. Caitriona, with Bess at her heels, followed close behind .

There was no rainbow now, but Caitriona had a picture firmly in her mind of the exact spot where the foot of the rainbow had rested, and she led Serge to the middle of the enclosure without the slightest hesitation.

'Dig,' she commanded.

Serge swept her a low bow. 'Yes, my lady,' he said, and they both laughed.

After about ten minutes' hard work, Serge leaned on his shovel and wiped his forehead.

'Ouf,' he said. 'Your Irish soil is very heavy, *n'est-ce pas?*'

'Stop talking French, and just dig,' said Caitriona, severely. Then she looked at him with concern. After all, he had been very ill.

'I'll have a go while you get your breath back,' she offered.

'No,' said Serge briefly. 'I am not tired.'

He dug for another few minutes in silence, and then gave a groan.

'Oh, no,' he said. 'Yet another stone.'

He carefully dug all around the stone, until it was completely bare of earth, and then stared at it in puzzlement. It was not a greenstone boulder, nor a block of cut limestone; it was a flat, smooth stone.

'It's a flagstone,' said Caitriona in surprise.

Quickly Serge picked up the shovel and began digging next to the flagstone, and soon they heard the ring of metal against stone. Once again Serge scraped it clear of earth. It was another flagstone, fitted closely to the first.

'It might be a floor,' he said excitedly. 'Maybe the floor of your castle. I'll try again.'

Caitriona clenched her hands in excitement while he dug for another few minutes. Then he leaned on his shovel and looked down. He had uncovered four enormous, flat flagstones.

'It must be a floor,' he said.

'Or a roof,' said Caitriona, with a sudden inspiration.

'But no crock of gold,' Serge said sadly.

'We haven't finished yet,' said Caitriona. She looked worriedly at him. He was sweating heavily and he had begun to look a little pale.

'We're not doing any more until you have a rest,' she said firmly. 'You sit on the stone over there, with Bess, and I'll run down and get you a drink of buttermilk.'

When she came back with the mug of buttermilk and a slice of soda-cake, she was glad to see that Serge's colour had come back. She sat beside him for a moment as he ate his cake, and then got up restlessly. Excitement was shooting through her, and she could not keep still. She picked up the shovel and started to dig around the edge of the first flagstone. The earth had been loosened by Serge, and it came away quite easily.

Just beside where Caitriona was digging, there was a big clump of marsh irises. Bess came over and tugged at it. For a while it stuck solidly, resisting her efforts, and then quite suddenly it loosened. Bess shook it like a rat and then went back and started to dig again, scattering earth in a shower behind her.

'Good girl, Bess,' encouraged Caitriona. 'Good girl! Dig, dig.'

Bess went on digging. Finally she stood back, panting. She looked at Caitriona and then at the ground. Caitriona moved over beside her and looked down.

There, just beside where the marsh irises had grown, was a hole.

'Serge!' Caitriona whispered, her voice almost lost with excitement. 'Look at this.'

'It is some steps, but they are blocked by that stone,' said Serge, joining her, his voice almost as excited as her own. 'Here, hold my cake.'

Dusting his hands and then spitting on them, Serge bent his back and hauled the large block of limestone out of the hole. Now they could see quite clearly that there was, indeed, a flight of steps leading down into the earth.

With shining eyes, they stared at each other.

'It must be the cave of your castle,' said Serge eventually.

'The cave?'

'No, I mean the cellar,' said Serge. 'We go down, yes?'

'We go down, yes,' teased Caitriona. 'But first we get a candle.'

Once again she ran down the hill to the cottage, with Bess galloping beside her. What will I say to Ma? she wondered. She really did not want to tell her stepmother anything until they had seen what was underground. What excuse could she make up for needing a candle?

She need not have worried, however. When she reached the house, she could hear Ann talking to Michael down by the pigsty. She must be feeding the pig, Caitriona thought. Quick as a flash, Caitriona dashed into the cottage, dragged a stool over to the little cupboard, climbed up on it, and took out a candle and her father's flint and tinder-box.

Almost tripping over Bess, she raced back up to the *cathair*. Her hands were trembling so much that it took her three attempts to get a spark from the flint, but eventually she managed it. Carefully she set fire to the tinder in the little metal box and lit the candle from its smouldering sparks. She handed the candle to Serge.

'You go first,' she said.

# CHAPTER NINE

The top step was broken, but the rest were sound, though slippery from the moss which covered them. Caitriona followed Serge cautiously, sliding each foot out in front of her until it rested on a firm surface.

'See the walls,' said Serge. 'They are made from the same stone — what is it your father called it?'

'Limestone,' said Caitriona, looking curiously at the blocks of stone; she could see them clearly in the light of the candle which Serge held up.

'You see, I am right,' continued Serge. 'See how well cut these blocks of limestone are. Each edge is as straight as if it were done with a ruler. These steps belong to this castle of yours.'

Caitriona could feel that her heart was beating quickly and unevenly. She could not speak; she felt as if she could hardly breathe. She stood stupidly staring at the blocks of limestone encrusted with the moss of centuries.

'Let's go on down,' said Serge. 'Look, there is a door.'

At the bottom of the steps was a small door, standing open. The top of it was shaped like an arch, and it was heavily studded with rusty iron nails.

'You see?' said Serge again. 'This is a very good door. It is very old, hundreds of years old, but it is still here after all those years.'

'Never mind about the door,' said Caitriona in a

queer husky voice, not like her own at all. 'Let's see what's inside.'

They both went through the door and stood just inside. They could not get in any further, because the whole room was full of smashed furniture, old books, and heaps of fallen stone and crushed masonry. Serge held the candle high so that its light showed the ceiling of the underground room.

'Look,' he said. 'You can see what happened. Look at the broken part of the roof. Something knocked your castle down — perhaps a cannon — and now only this souterrain remains .'

'What does "souterrain" mean?' asked Caitriona, her eyes wandering over the broken tables and chairs and the blocks of stone.

'It is an underground room,' explained Serge. 'Most of these things were probably in the rooms upstairs; when the castle fell down, a hole was smashed in the roof of the souterrain, and these things fell through.'

Caitriona looked around the little room. The three sides nearest to her were made from squared-off blocks of limestone, but the fourth wall was made from the heavy, irregular greenstone boulders which had been used in the walls of her own cottage and in all the field walls on the farm. There was a small gap in that far wall, but it was blocked by earth.

'It is funny, that,' said Serge. 'You would think that all the walls would be made the same. Perhaps that wall was part of a still more ancient place.'

'Let's go across,' said Caitriona. 'We can climb over the furniture.'

'No,' said Serge urgently, grasping her sleeve and

holding her back. 'No, it is too dangerous. The middle of that roof looks not safe. The slightest movement could bring everything crashing down on us. We must stay by the door.'

Caitriona could see the sense in what he said. She knew that the weight of the massive flagstones which lined the roof would be enough to kill a grown man. She bent down, picked up some pieces of old books and threw them behind her, wondering if anything might be buried beneath them.

'You look for your crock of gold, no?' said Serge, amused.

'Yes,' said Caitriona, firmly.

Serge picked up one of the pages which she had thrown aside, and his expression changed.

'Stop,' he said quickly. 'Be careful.' He seized the next book from her hands and cried, '*Oh là là, quel livre merveilleux!*'

'I told you, stop talking French,' grunted Caitriona, trying to shift a heavy chair without actually stepping into the underground room. She was beginning to feel a little uneasy. She was not as sure of finding the crock of gold as she had pretended. This room just looked full of old junk.

She peered under the chair. There was a box lying there. It was not made of gold — in fact, it was made of some dull, dark grey metal — but through the dirt and dust, Caitriona could see that the lid was covered in a strange pattern of interlacing lines. Perhaps there might be something inside ....

With a hard jerk, she managed to shift the chair a little more. She reached down and pulled out the box.

Using a piece of broken wood, she managed to clear the dirt from the lid, so that the pattern stood out clearly.

'Feel how heavy it is, Serge,' said Caitriona. 'There must be something valuable in it!'

Serge carefully placed the book which he was holding on the step behind him, and took the box from Caitriona's hands.

'Don't be too hopeful,' he warned. 'This box is made of lead and that is a very heavy metal. It is possible that there is nothing inside.'

There was a lock on the old box, but it had been broken many long years ago, so Serge had little difficulty in opening the box, once he had dug away the dirt of centuries from around its lid. Caitriona held her breath while he opened it — and then let it out in a deep sigh of disappointment.

Inside the box was yet another old book — and this was not even as beautiful as the book which Serge had been holding, and only half the size. She opened it. It had no pictures; it was filled with writing, the letters a strange shape and the words unfamiliar.

'That is written in Latin,' said Serge, looking over her shoulder.

'Oh,' said Caitriona. She put the book back in the box. She could hardly bear the disappointment. She had been so sure there would be something valuable here ...

Caitriona felt the tears welling up in her eyes. She went back up the steps, to where Bess was waiting patiently. It was nice to be out in the air again, and to feel the sun on her back. She knelt on the ground, put her arms around Bess's neck, and leaned against the silky head; and then she heard Serge call.

'Caitriona!' he shouted. 'Where are you?'

Caitriona tried to say something, but she couldn't. Her throat was swollen and she felt as if she could not utter a word.

In a couple of minutes, she heard Serge come up the steps. He stood beside her, offering her his beautiful linen handkerchief. Caitriona was too ashamed to touch it; she pretended not to see it and turned away, wiping her eyes on the hem of her petticoat when she thought Serge was not looking. She knew that he was wondering what to say, so she made a great effort and said, 'I'm all right now. It was stupid, but I did think we might find something valuable. I'm quite excited about it all the same. Wait until Da gets home! He'll be amazed.'

'Look, Caitriona,' said Serge. 'Don't give up hope. We *have* found something valuable. Let's sit on this stone and look at the book.'

Caitriona sat on the stone and Serge sat beside her. He put the lead box containing the plain book on the ground beside them; then he opened the old book which Caitriona had thrown down, and carefully turned over the pages.

The book was stained with damp and smelt mouldy. The cover was torn and the first few pages hard to read, but the centre was full of brightly-coloured pictures and wonderfully-illuminated writing. Caitriona began to look at it with more interest. One page especially took her fancy: it had a huge capital M on it, and between the upright bars of the letter peered the face of a strange cream-coloured cat with bright blue eyes. It was beautifully done. Caitriona had never seen anything like it.

'Do you really think it's valuable?' she asked doubtfully.

Serge turned the book over, handling the torn cover with the utmost care.

'I do,' he said. 'I am wondering how old it is. Let's see. If I can peel these two pages apart, I might find out more about it.'

The two front pages were stuck together with damp, but Serge managed to prise them apart; and there was the title page.

'The Psalter of King David,' he read. 'Copied by Malachy of Kilfenora, in the year of Our Lord 1286.'

'The year 1286!' said Caitriona, astonished. 'But that's more than five hundred years ago. This book is more than five hundred years old. Perhaps it is valuable, after all.'

'And look: under "Malachy of Kilfenora" is written "and of Drumshee". I wonder who he was, this Malachy of Kilfenora and of Drumshee.'

'Let's look at the other book,' said Caitriona. 'The one in the lead box. That might tell us some more about him. That one's in better condition. The box kept it dry.'

Serge picked up the book and turned over the pages in silence. There were no pictures in it, no fancy first letters, but it was written in the same small, square writing. Serge looked at the first page, translating the Latin slowly and hesitantly.

'It says, "This book is the story of my life, the life of Malachy of Drumshee."' Serge broke off and looked at Caitriona. 'You can see that he calls himself

"Malachy of Drumshee" now; he doesn't mention Kilfenora. Perhaps that means he came from Kilfenora and then settled here at Drumshee.'

'Read me some more,' said Caitriona impatiently.

Serge knitted his brows over the unfamiliar Latin, and continued.

'"— And also of Mary, my wife, and of Rory, my wife's brother, and of our great quest which ended so happily for all three of us."'

Caitriona began to feel excited. It was interesting, having this voice from the past talking to them.

'Let me look,' she said.

Once again she looked through the pages, and this time she found a picture, at the back of the book. It was just drawn in ink, not coloured, but it was a picture of something which Caitriona knew very well: the east face of the High Cross which stood in a field to the west of the Kilfenora cathedral. At the bottom of the page was some more writing in Latin.

Caitriona handed the book back to Serge.

'What does that say?' she asked urgently.

Serge peered at it, muttering to himself in French, and then said hesitantly, 'I think that it says: "The secret of the hidden purse of gold was carved into the stone at the bottom of the High Cross."'

# CHAPTER TEN

When Tom came back that evening with the news that Serge's letter was on its way to France, he was greeted with a scene of great excitement. Ann was using some stale bread to try and clean some of the mildew stains from the precious book, and Serge and Caitriona were sitting under the lamp trying to wrestle the meaning from Malachy's life story. Caitriona knew no Latin whatsoever, and Serge had not studied it since he was a schoolboy, so they were not getting on very fast.

Tom looked at the back page of the little book with interest.

'A purse of gold,' he said. 'Still, I wouldn't be too sure about it, Caitriona. After all, that was five hundred years ago. I expect somebody has dug it up by now.'

'Look at the other book, Monsieur McMahon,' said Serge, putting aside his translation with some relief. 'Look at the beauty of it. Even though the outside is ruined, this should get you much money.'

'It's very beautiful,' said Tom, picking up the Psalter of King David and turning over its pages slowly and reverently. 'I don't know about getting money for it, though. I don't know where I would go.'

'You could go to Galway, Da,' said Caitriona impatiently. 'If you got a lot of money for it, then there would be enough for me to —' She stopped. Her stepmother was eyeing her grimly.

'For you? Why you, may I ask? What about the rest of us?'

'I only meant — enough for me to be trained as a singer,' mumbled Caitriona.

Tom sat on the big chair by the chimney and looked from his daughter to his wife.

'What's all this about?' he asked quietly.

'I want to be a singer,' said Caitriona, looking directly at her father, and avoiding her stepmother's angry eyes. 'I want to be a singer and I want to be trained properly. Serge's mother could train me, but it takes money. She isn't rich, and she has Serge's sisters to look after. I'd need money. I'd have to be able to pay for my food and my clothes and my singing lessons.'

'Lord bless us and save us,' said Tom. 'Where did all this come from?'

'I think I started thinking about it that night I sang for Mr Quin and he said I should go to London or Paris to get my voice trained,' said Caitriona, meeting his eyes courageously. 'I put it out of my head, because I knew it was impossible. And then Serge began telling me about his mother, and all the girls she teaches singing to, so I began to think about it again. But I'll need money ....' Her voice tailed away. She felt close to tears. 'I don't want to take anything from you and Ma and Michael, but I just wish there was enough money to go around, so I could do that.'

'Well,' said her father slowly, 'I'll tell you what. I'll get the best price I can for this book, and then, when we see how much that is, we can talk about all this again. And I'll tell you what,' he added lightly. 'If you and Serge manage to work out the secret of the purse of gold in that little book there — well, that will be for you to keep for yourself.'

'Oh, Da!' cried Caitriona, rushing to hug him. Out of the corner of her eye she could see that Ann's grim expression had relaxed; she was even half-smiling. No one believes in this purse of gold, thought Caitriona. Not even Serge, really. He's more interested in the Psalter of King David.

Resolutely she went back to the little book. She turned to the last page and stared at the picture of the cross.

It was strange: there was a shape, at the bottom of the cross, which looked as if it had been added as an afterthought to the intricate designs at the top. It looks like a little opening, perhaps, Caitriona thought doubtfully; but an opening to what? A cave, perhaps?

She turned to the front of the book. Yes, it said 'Malachy of Drumshee' there, although it said 'Malachy of Kilfenora and of Drumshee' in the Psalter of King David.

'Serge, do you think the purse of gold is buried at Kilfenora or at Drumshee?' she asked.

Serge put down the Psalter of King David reluctantly and came across to Caitriona.

'I am not sure,' he said honestly. 'I am so — how do you say? — so rusty with the tongue Latin that I am very slow with this book. It is written like a story about when this man Malachy was young; and he has two friends, Rory and Mary.'

'Yes, but is there anything about gold in it?' asked Caitriona impatiently.

'Yes,' replied Serge. 'In the beginning of the book, Rory tells a story about the hidden treasure of Kilfenora.

I must study it longer; then I may find out more.'

'Why don't you start at the end?' said Caitriona, in despair, after Serge had muttered to himself for about ten minutes and had not yet even finished the first page. 'It's going to take you years to get through the whole book, and I can't wait years! You'll be gone soon, and I don't know anyone else who knows Latin, so the secret will be lost forever.'

'Good idea,' said Serge good-humouredly, turning to the last page.

'Don't murder the lad, Caitriona,' said Tom. 'He's doing his best. Be reasonable, now. The chances of a purse of gold hanging around for five hundred years, in a poor place like this, aren't very high. Don't set your heart on it. I was only joking; I didn't really think you'd find it. '

'What does the last page say?' asked Caitriona feverishly, ignoring her father and focusing on Serge.

Serge muttered some more to himself, looking up at the ceiling for inspiration and then back down at the page. At last, just as Caitriona felt that she would scream with impatience, he spoke.

'I don't know if this book will be of much importance to us, Caitriona. This Malachy says that he and his friends had such excitement in looking for the treasure that he wanted to leave a puzzle for some boy or girl in the future, and he hoped that they would feel the same excitement in discovering the purse of gold. He says that the secret of the hiding-place was carved by Rory onto the east face of the High Cross which stands in the field to the west of the abbey.'

'That means west of the cathedral,' said Tom,

listening with interest. 'I've heard there was an abbey of monks there, once.'

Caitriona looked up, her face full of resolution. 'Tomorrow is Sunday,' she said. 'Let's go to mass in Kilfenora, and Serge and I can have a look at the High Cross. There might be something on it that could help us make sense of the puzzle.'

'That's dangerous,' objected Ann. 'Someone might guess that Serge is French.'

'I think it's more dangerous to keep him hidden here all the time,' said Caitriona. 'People are wondering why they never see him. Joe O'Donoghue was asking me about him the other day, and I had to say he wasn't very well. He'll just have to hang his head and mutter and pretend to be shy. He looks quite ordinary in your old clothes, Da; and before mass, if we get there early enough, you can get him to sing a song. He sounds completely Irish when he sings.'

Tom nodded his head. 'There's some sense in that,' he said. 'That's what we'll do. Sing that song about going to the fair for me, lad. I'll listen carefully and see if I can fault you.'

Caitriona listened for the first few lines, but it seemed faultless to her, so her mind drifted away. She heard the beginnings of a whimper from the inner room; Michael was just starting to wake up. Caitriona picked him out of his truckle-bed and sat on the big bed, holding him in her arms and kissing his sleepy, hot little face. Did she really want to leave Michael and her father and the farm at Drumshee?

I don't know, she thought. I just don't know.

'Come on, Michael,' she said aloud. 'Let's go and find Bess. We can ask her what she thinks.'

# CHAPTER ELEVEN

Next morning there was even more bustle than usual as the family got ready for mass. For once Caitriona did not object to having her damp hair twisted into spirals around pieces of screwed-up paper and tied with rags. By the time the milking was done, her hair was dry; and when the rags and paper were taken out, it was curled into elegant ringlets. She put on her best dress and tied her sash around her waist; for once, she did not hitch her skirt up over the sash. By the time she was ready, she looked like quite an elegant young lady.

Serge was already ready and waiting outside the cottage. Caitriona was glad to see that he looked quite Irish. Tom had cut his hair the night before, and that had completely changed his appearance. He looked at Caitriona admiringly. *'Oh la la!'* he said. *'Bien jolie, n'est-ce pas?'*

'Stop talking French. Practise saying *Dia 's Muire dhuit*,' she commanded, feeling a little shy in the face of his admiration.

*'Dia 's Muire dhuit,'* Serge said obediently. Caitriona listened critically, her head on one side, trying to imagine what it might sound like to a stranger.

'You'll do,' she said, feeling rather guilty about all the time they had spent chatting in English when she should have been forcing Serge to talk Irish.

At that moment, Tom, Ann and little Michael came out of the cottage, all dressed in their Sunday best. Ann looked tense and pale, and Tom went off, without a word, to harness the horse to the cart.

I hope it will be all right, thought Caitriona, beginning to feel rather tense herself.

For the whole of the three miles to Kilfenora, she chatted resolutely in Irish to Serge, not allowing him to say a single word in English. Who knows who might be listening from behind the hedge? she thought.

They arrived at the chapel with plenty of time to spare. To Caitriona's pleasure, there in front of the chapel, with a crowd of people around him, was old Mr Quin.

Clenching her hands in an effort to overcome her nervousness, she went straight across to him. Out of the corner of her eye, she could see her father tying up the horse in front of Culliney's Inn. She advanced upon Mr Quin, smiling as winningly as she could.

'Well, if it isn't Caitriona,' said Mr Quin. There was such pleasure in his voice that Caitriona felt guilty, remembering how much she had once hated him. 'I hear you and your father had great adventures, being lost at sea and landing up the west coast. Tell me now, did ye see any of the French at all?'

Caitriona's blood ran cold. She did not dare trust her voice to say anything, but she shook her head with her best smile. She was beginning to feel the muscles of her cheeks ache with the effort of holding that smile.

'Well, what about giving us a song, then?' said Mr Quin, as Caitriona had known he would. 'What are you going to sing for us?'

Caitriona pretended to hesitate for a moment, to give her father a chance to come over with Serge.

'I'll sing "There's a fair tomorrow",' she said. 'There's my cousin Patrick, from the north, coming over with my father. I'll get him to sing it with me. He's got a great voice, but he's very shy. You'd never get a word out of him if it wasn't for the singing.'

As soon as her father and Serge joined them, Caitriona said quickly, 'Get out your pipe, Da, we're going to sing "There's a fair tomorrow". Come on, Patrick, you sing with me.'

Serge, she noted with satisfaction, was playing his part to perfection, peeping under his eyelashes like a bashful country lad and turning his cap over and over in his hands. As they sang together, Caitriona could hear that his singing voice sounded completely Irish.

As soon as the song was over and everyone was murmuring compliments, she caught Serge by the hand.

'I want to show Patrick around Kilfenora, Da,' she said to her father. 'We'll be back in plenty of time for mass. We'll come as soon as we hear the bell.'

'Ouf!' said Serge, as they went up the little curved street.

'Talk Irish,' Caitriona hissed warningly.

The cathedral of Kilfenora was where the Protestants went on Sunday. A few well-dressed gentlemen, with powdered wigs and white breeches, were handing their ladies out of carriages in front of the doors of the ancient church. For a moment Caitriona stared enviously at the laces and silks and furs these grand ladies wore; but then, tugging Serge by the hand again, she led him around the back of the cathedral, towards the field where the High Cross stood.

'I suppose it has been here for five hundred years,' said Serge, speaking Irish carefully and slowly.

'I suppose so,' said Caitriona, looking up at the cross. 'It looks just the same as it did in the little book, doesn't it?' she added in a low tone.

She gave a quick look around, but no one was watching. All the Catholics were standing in front of Culliney's, gossiping, and all the Protestants were in front of the cathedral. Caitriona quickly hitched up her skirt, letting it blouse out over her sash, and knelt on the grass to examine the bottom of the cross.

It did look the same as it had looked in Malachy's little book; but there was one difference. Leading from the patterned area of the cross down to the triangular shape at the very bottom was something which looked like a rope; and beside this rope, deeply cut into the stone, were two figures and a word. It was very hard to be certain of the figures, as they were blurred by the lichens which grew all over the cross, but Caitriona scratched and tore at the stone with her sharp fingernails until she had scraped the spot clean.

Serge knelt beside her, and together they looked at the two figures.

'Fifty-five,' murmured Caitriona.

Serge nodded. 'Fifty-five paces,' he said. 'That word, *passus*, means "paces".'

'What could it be?' whispered Caitriona. 'What does it look like to you?'

'To me, it looks like a bell hanging from a rope,' Serge whispered back.

'Yes, it does to me, too,' said Caitriona, forgetting, in her excitement, to whisper. 'But if it was a bell-rope, what would be the point of putting down that measurement? It must mean fifty-five paces from somewhere — from here, I suppose, where the cross is.'

'Let's try it,' said Serge, in very bad Irish.

'You go to the west and I'll go to the east,' said Caitriona. 'It's almost time for mass; we must hurry.'

Counting carefully, Caitriona paced out fifty-five steps, stretching her legs as much as possible in order to make sure that her steps were as long as a grown man's. When she finished, she was in the middle of the field. She could see all the fine ladies and gentlemen standing in front of the cathedral, and she hoped that they would not wonder what she was doing.

Serge came across to her.

'I have tried the fifty-five paces west,' he whispered. 'I have found nothing significant.'

'You do the north next, and I'll do the south,' Caitriona whispered back.

She had just finished the pacing when the bell rang for mass, and she signalled to Serge to follow her to the chapel. She did not need to ask him whether he had found anything interesting; his expression told her that he had had as little luck as she had.

As they entered the chapel, Caitriona saw Serge look around in surprise. Probably the churches in France are very fine, she thought, not just a big room with whitewashed walls and a rough earthen floor. She nudged Serge, to show him where Tom was standing, and she herself joined Ann and Michael on the women's side of the church.

Throughout the introductory prayers, as Caitriona

knelt with her face in her hands, she kept wondering what they should do. The purse of gold could be buried anywhere in the field, fifty-five paces from the cross, she supposed; and then again, that clue on the bottom of the cross might mean something completely different .... Absent-mindedly she stood for the gospel, with her mind still on the problem, and then sat down for the sermon.

The priest's first words, however, jerked Caitriona out of her abstraction. Father Charles Carrigg was new to the parish, and he was not at all like the timid little man who had been there before. He spoke like Serge did. He spoke of freedom and of self-respect, of the Irish people's right to own their own property, their own country; to have their own schools; to pay their dues to their own clergy and to none other. Beside her, Caitriona felt her stepmother stiffen. All around the church, people were glancing at one another — mostly with fear in their eyes, although a few were blazing with excitement.

The sermon ended. Surely, Caitriona thought, that was the most unusual sermon ever heard in this church! The priest crossed himself and was turning to go back to the altar, when the door at the end of the chapel was flung open and a detachment of soldiers clattered into the church.

A few people screamed, and children howled. Everyone leaped to their feet and many of those at the back of the church tried to get out, pushing and shoving, all trying to squeeze through the door at the same time. Caitriona glanced across at Serge, her face white with shock, and was relieved to see him, and Tom beside him, staring stolidly ahead.

She looked back at the altar. Father Carrigg had turned around again; he stood at the foot of the altar steps, looking calmly at the soldiers. As they marched up toward him, he slipped off the sacred mass vestments, slowly and deliberately. With his eyes still fixed on the soldiers, he handed them to the altar boys and advanced towards the soldiers.

'Is it me you want?' he asked calmly.

The soldiers swore at him and tied his hands with rope, and then some of them dragged him out.

The captain walked up the steps and shouted: 'Out of this church in two minutes, all you filthy Irish scum! If any one of you is left after I count two hundred, you'll spend the night in Ennis jail alongside your precious priest.'

He began to count as the terrified people streamed out of the chapel. Caitriona could see that her father and Serge were standing quietly together at the bottom of the chapel, waiting for them. Neither showed any fear, and Caitriona felt proud of them both.

'It's all right, Michael,' she said encouragingly, as they passed the soldiers. 'Don't cry. It's a nice quick mass today. We'll go home now, and you can play with Bess.'

'And with Serge?' said Michael, smiling through his tears.

Caitriona's heart gave a sudden leap inside her chest. She looked apprehensively at the nearest soldier, but he had not even looked at them. She smiled to herself. Michael was not very good at talking, and very few people, other than his family, could understand him. In his baby voice, 'Serge' sounded more like 'third'.

'Well,' said Tom, as they joined him, 'there was only one person who came out of that chapel today with a smile on her face, and that was my brave girl. Well done. We're not afraid, are we? Get in the cart now, and off we go back to Drumshee.'

Serge said nothing, but he smiled at Caitriona, and as they climbed into the cart he whispered, 'Bravo.' Caitriona felt quite proud of herself. It was like being on board the French ship again. She sat at the back of the cart with her head held high and thought how lovely it would be if everyone cheered as she went along. Perhaps one day, when she was a famous singer, they might.

Her glance picked out the High Cross as they went along, and her spirits fell slightly. They had not achieved much that day, and now she would never dare to bring Serge into Kilfenora again.

# CHAPTER TWELVE

A month went by, and during the whole of that time, Caitriona and Serge continued to think about the purse of gold. Every evening, when the work on the farm was finished, Serge sat under the lamp and read aloud — hesitantly at first, but then more confidently — from the story of Malachy and Mary and Rory. Listening to him was as good as a play, declared Tom; and time after time he let his pipe go out while he listened, open-mouthed, to the exciting adventure .

They found no new clues, however, to the whereabouts of the purse of gold. In every spare moment that she had, Caitriona climbed on a stool, took down the lead box from the little cupboard in the chimney wall, and studied the last page of the book. Now she could see what she had missed the first time. In figures so tiny that she only spotted them when a shaft of sunlight lit up the book one afternoon, '55' was written beside the moulding on the cross. It had to be fifty-five paces from the cross; there could be no other meaning.

'Perhaps if we went over to Kilfenora and dug a circle around the cross, just fifty-five paces out from it, we might find the purse of gold,' she said to her father one day.

Tom paused in his work of shovelling the potatoes into the deep straw-lined pit which would keep them safe from rats and crows in the winter, and looked at her in astonishment.

'Are you mad?' he said. 'How in heaven's name could I do a thing like that? Anyway, you'd have to dig up half the field before you found it, even if you were sure it was there. One man's pace isn't the same as another man's pace. And how could I do a thing like that to another man's field?'

Caitriona scowled, but made no reply. It was impossible. She knew that. There must be some other meaning to that '55', she thought crossly.

In the meantime, she and Serge got on with clearing the souterrain. 'Save anything that I could use,' Tom had ordered; so they piled up all the usable bits of furniture — table-legs and chair-legs, a piece of an old dresser, some shelving — in one corner of the souterrain, just beside some tall old pots which, by some miracle, had escaped being broken.

'These pots will be great,' said Tom, when he came down to see their work. 'I'll use them for storing the oats. I had a great crop this year. I'll sow some more next year, now that I know we have somewhere to store them during the winter. I never like to rely on the potatoes too much.'

'We're making a lovely room of it,' said Caitriona, surveying it with satisfaction. 'It would make a lovely secret hiding-place.'

'It would be a good place for me to hide,' said Serge seriously. 'If ever the soldiers came, I could hide here and you could put a flagstone over the entrance.'

Tom nodded and went back to his work. He said nothing at the time, but evidently he thought about what Serge had said; that evening, he said, 'Listen, Ann, and you, Caitriona; even after Serge is gone, I

think we should keep that place the lad calls the souterrain a secret.'

His wife looked at him in surprise, and he continued. 'These are troublesome times, and there'll be more of them. You never know when we might need a secret place to hide ourselves or our stores.'

'I'm sure you're right,' said Ann slowly, turning the matter over in her mind and nodding her head thoughtfully.

'So that's settled,' said Tom. 'The secret must be kept between the three of us, and when Michael is six or seven years old — whenever he has the sense to keep quiet — we'll tell him. Then he can tell his children and the secret will always be kept, just by the McMahons, as long as there are McMahons at Drumshee.'

The next day, Serge and Caitriona began work again on the souterrain. Serge was working very fast, Caitriona noticed. He had not said anything, but Caitriona knew that every day he expected to hear from his mother; and he seemed to want this job to be done before he left Drumshee.

Caitriona could hardly bear to think of him going, so she also concentrated on working as hard as she could. By the middle of the morning, only a small pile of rubbish was left in the corner of the souterrain. Caitriona went over and started to sort it out: pieces of wood for burning on the kitchen fire in one pile, rubbish to be burnt on the bonfire in another pile, and anything to be kept in a third. It was mainly rubbish, after she had picked out the bigger pieces of wood, so she picked up the broom and began to sweep what was left into a pile.

As she did so, something rolled away. Bess pounced on it, picked it up in her mouth and offered it to Caitriona. It was a tiny metal vase. Caitriona dropped the broom and scrubbed at it with an old rag. Its smooth surface was engraved with some lines or patterns.

'Good girl, Bess,' she said. 'Serge, look at this. It's beautiful. Look at all the little engravings on it.'

'Bring it out to the light,' said Serge, hoisting a pile of wood onto his shoulder. 'Walk behind me and make sure I do not drop anything,' he added.

Caitriona followed him up the steep steps, now cleaned of the moss and slime of centuries. She was so used to going up and down them, now, that she knew every hollow in them. When they reached the top, she scrubbed at the little vase again; a gleam from the late October sun shone on it, picking out the deep sheen of the metal.

'That's bronze,' said Serge. 'It is a lovely little vase. Go and offer it to your mother. She can keep flowers in it.'

'She isn't my mother,' said Caitriona, busily polishing the tiny vase and not looking at him. 'I would have thought you'd know that. You can see the difference between the way she treats me and the way she treats Michael.'

'*Oh là là,*' said Serge, sitting down on a boulder. 'What is the matter?'

'Well, she's not,' said Caitriona sullenly. 'I wish my real mother was alive.'

Serge laughed, and Caitriona looked at him angrily.

'I am not really laughing at you,' he said quickly.

'But my sister Aimée, who is the same age as you — she talks just like you. Her mother is her real mother, but they argue all day long and Aimée always says that Michelle is the favourite.'

Caitriona smiled a little. She wished she could meet Aimée and talk about mothers with her.

She looked down at the little vase and made up her mind.

'All right,' she said. 'I'll bring it down and give it to her.'

When Caitriona arrived at the door of the cottage, Michael was asleep under a tree and Ann was taking the opportunity to indulge in one of her orgies of cleaning. Every piece of furniture was out in the yard, and Caitriona could hear the sound of flag-stones being scrubbed inside the cottage. She stood awkwardly at the door, the little vase in her hand, while Bess cowered behind her legs.

Ann looked up. 'Well,' she said sharply, 'what do you want?'

'Would you like this vase, for keeping flowers in?'

Ann wiped her face with the hem of her apron and sniffed. 'As if I hadn't enough things to dust as it is,' she said. 'Take it away and throw it on the bonfire. And hurry up and finish up there. I could do with some help here.'

Without answering, Caitriona ran back up to the *cathair*.

'She doesn't want it,' she told Serge. 'She says to throw it on the bonfire.'

'Oh, no,' said Serge. 'You must not do that. It is too beautiful. Can you keep it in your bedroom?'

'I'd better not,' said Caitriona briefly. She looked

at the little vase. It did seem a pity to throw it away.

Her face brightened. 'I know,' she said. 'I'll keep it in the shrine, in front of the statue of St Brigid. Have you seen the little shrine, Serge? Come and have a look. It's down by the cattle drinking place.'

'It is hidden, no?'

'Yes,' said Caitriona. 'It's hidden under that big old ash tree.'

The two of them went down to the cattle drinking place and pushed their way through the thick branches of the ash. Serge lifted the little stone statue out of its wedge-shaped house and turned it over admiringly in his hands.

'It is very old, no?' he said.

'Yes,' said Caitriona automatically, and then corrected herself. 'At least, I suppose it's very old. I don't know, really. St Brigid was very old. She was around the time of St Patrick, I think — about a thousand years ago, or maybe more,' she ended vaguely.

'Older than that, I think,' said Serge thoughtfully, replacing the statue.

'You go back,' said Caitriona. 'I'll follow you in a moment. I just want to put some flowers in the vase.'

Carefully she filled the tiny bronze vase with clean water from the well; then she gathered a few late flowers of purple knapweed, and some deep blue scabious, and arranged them in front of the stone statue.

She peered out through the branches to make sure that Serge had really gone. Then she knelt down in front of the little wedge-shaped shrine.

'Please, St Brigid, help me to find that purse of

gold and to go to France and be trained as a singer,'
she whispered.

She got to her feet, admiring the perfect little vase.
It looks just right there, she thought; she was glad
that her stepmother had rejected it. Caitriona resolved to keep fresh flowers or leaves in it all year
round. Then, feeling more cheerful, she went back to
finish her sweeping.

# CHAPTER THIRTEEN

Caitriona went to sleep that night with the same prayer on her lips, but when she woke up, she felt very depressed. It seemed impossible that she would ever find the purse of gold. She would be stuck at home for the rest of her life.

She put on her worst gown, dragged a comb through her hair and came downstairs with her head hanging and her heart heavy inside her. Even Ann noticed how quiet Caitriona was during breakfast and urged her to have some more to eat, and Tom tried to joke her out of her bad mood; but nothing, Caitriona felt, could cheer her up again. She felt as if she was going to be miserable forever.

In the end, Tom got up and said to Michael, 'I think I'd better not take old Misery to see Uncle Ned, what do you think, son? Her long face would only depress him.'

'Uncle Ned,' echoed Michael, banging his spoon on the table. Caitriona looked up with excitement, her depression suddenly beginning to melt away.

'Oh, Da, are you going to Liscannor?'

Her father laughed. 'That livened you up. Yes, I think I'd better fetch the old cart back. I have to deliver some potatoes to Ennistymon. I thought we could take both the horses down, one of them tied to the back of the cart, and then you could drive one of the carts back. Would you be able to manage that, do you think?'

Caitriona ignored this. He knew perfectly well that she was able to drive the cart. 'When are you going, Da?' she asked.

'I thought I might go today,' he replied. 'There's not much to do now I've finished the potatoes, and anyway, Serge is expecting to hear from his uncle any day now. There might be a message waiting for us at Liscannor.'

'I'll get ready straight away,' said Caitriona, and rushed up to her bedroom in the loft. As she brushed her hair and changed her gown, she thought of the last time she and her father had gone to Liscannor — of the great adventure they had had. Perhaps something else exciting will happen today, she thought, as she ran down the wooden ladder from her bedroom.

When they arrived at Liscannor, Uncle Ned came out to meet them.

'Well, glory be to God! I'm glad to see you,' he said. 'I was just going to find someone to take a message for me over to Drumshee. Come in, come in,' he added, with a hasty look around him.

It was only when they were safely inside the cottage, and both halves of the door were shut, that Uncle Ned told them his news. Even then, he lowered his voice before he spoke.

'They're here,' he said. 'All three of them — the mother and the two sisters. They came over with her brother, the sea captain, the lad's uncle. They've come across to bring him home.'

'Well!' said Tom. 'What in the blazes made her do that?'

'The way I heard the story, she thought it would be safer for the boy if she and the girls were with him. After all, who would ever think of a French soldier with three women with him?'

'Well, there might be something in that,' said Tom. 'I was worrying a bit myself, in case French boats might be searched on their way in or out. You know, it's a pity I didn't bring Serge with me. We could have just put him on the ship today, and that would have been the end of that. I know Ann's worried about having him in the house, ever since that business at Kilfenora church when they arrested Father Carrigg.'

'I heard about that,' said Ned, looking grave. 'That was a bad business. But it would have been no good you bringing the lad down today. They can't leave for a few more days; the captain has all his trading to see to, and he daren't do anything different or the English soldiers will be down on him. No, the women are going to wait on board, and they'll sail a week from tomorrow, or before.'

Caitriona could feel excitement running through her, shooting little spurts through her veins. She caught her father's sleeve.

'Da, let's go and see them!' she implored. 'There wouldn't be any harm in that.'

Tom looked hesitantly at Ned. 'What do you think? Would it do any harm?'

'Divil a bit,' said Ned. 'Divil a bit. Just take a stroll down to the quay. You'll know the ship; it's the one with big brown sails and some French name on it.'

'We'll leave the horses here, then,' said Tom, rising to his feet. 'We'll walk down and have a word with the lad's mother. Caitriona's picked up a bit of French from Serge, so she might be able to talk to her. The woman will want to know all about her son.'

'She can talk English,' said Caitriona. 'Serge told me. She taught him his English.'

There was only one ship tied up at the quay. Its sails were brown, and the name painted on its side was *Marie Rose*. Caitriona looked at her father and he nodded. No one was about, so they walked up the gangway, climbed on board, and then looked about uncertainly.

As they were wondering what to do, Caitriona saw a girl peeping out of a doorway. She was about Caitriona's age, although she was smaller; she had lovely yellow hair, the colour of primroses, and big blue eyes, and she was dressed very fashionably in sprigged muslin.

The two girls stared at each other for a moment. Then the door opened wider, and out came an elegant lady, so like Serge that Caitriona knew at once that she was his mother. Without any trace of her usual shyness, Caitriona went up to her, curtsied and said in her very best French:

*'Bonjour, Madame. Votre fils Serge va très bien.'*

'And you must be Caitriona,' said the lady, speaking excellent English, much to Caitriona's relief. 'And you are Monsieur McMahon,' she added, giving Tom her hand. 'Come in, come in, we are quite alone; all the men have gone to unload the ship. This is my daughter Aimée, who is thirteen years old, and this is Michelle, who is eleven.'

Michelle was as dark as Aimée was fair. She seemed very shy — she smiled, but said nothing — but Aimée was very friendly.

'We have heard much things about you from my brother,' she said, seizing Caitriona by the hand. 'Come down to my cabin and tell me about you.'

'But first, some wine and some cake,' said Madame Dupont. 'While you drink, you can tell me about Serge.'

Caitriona took a cautious sip of the wine, and her eyes widened. She had never tasted anything like it in her life. Warm colour came into her usually pale cheeks, and she felt as if liquid fire was bubbling in her veins. She looked at Aimée and smiled.

'We go to my cabin now,' said Aimée.

'Ah, but first you must sing for us, Caitriona,' said Madame Dupont. 'Serge, he say that you have the voice of an angel.'

'I'll hum you a note, Caitriona,' said Tom. He was stretched out in a chair and he looked as if he, too, was enjoying the wine.

This is my chance, thought Caitriona. She's just asking me to sing so as to be polite, but I'll show her that I am good.

She got up and stood the way Mr Quin had taught her: shoulders pulled back, head held high, and her hands loosely clasped in front of her. She felt a great sense of power, an absolute certainty that she could, indeed, impress Serge's mother.

When she finished singing, there was a moment's silence. Then Madame Dupont said: '*Magnifique!*'

That was all she said; but she said it so thoughtfully that Caitriona was quite satisfied.

Caitriona smiled at Aimée again. Aimée seemed a bit stunned; she blinked and said, 'But you are better than me.'

Caitriona hid a smile. 'I'm sure I'm not,' she said quickly. She badly wanted to be friends with Aimée. 'Will we go and see your cabin now?'

'*Oui, oui, allez-y, mes enfants,*' commanded Madame Dupont.

Michelle tried to follow as well, but Aimée pushed her back and muttered something in French to her. Caitriona felt a little sorry for Michelle; but, she thought as she looked around Aimée's cabin, it's so small that there would hardly have been room for a third person anyway. She sat on the bed and looked admiringly at Aimée's primrose-coloured hair and cornflower-blue eyes.

'I think you're very pretty,' she said.

'And you also,' said Aimée in careful English.

'Where did you all learn to speak English?' asked Caitriona.

'My grandmother is English, and she learn us all to speak very good,' said Aimée proudly.

'Do you like being on the ship?' asked Caitriona.

'No, I hate it! It is horrible — I am always quarrelling with my mother and my sister. And now we must spend another few days shut up here!'

Caitriona had a sudden inspiration.

'Would you like to come back to Drumshee with me? You could stay for a few days, and then we'd bring you back with Serge. You could share my bedroom, and I'd show you everything .... Do come!'

# CHAPTER FOURTEEN

On the way back to Drumshee, Caitriona almost had to pinch herself to see whether she was dreaming. There was Aimée, sitting beside her in the new cart; and, best of all, before they left the ship, Madame Dupont had asked Caitriona to sing again, and then tested her with different notes. Afterwards, she had drawn Tom aside and had a long, whispered conversation with him. Caitriona kept remembering how pleased Madame Dupont had looked, and she tried not to let herself think about how sad her father's face had been after that conversation, and how silent he had been ever since. She chatted away to Aimée, and Aimée chattered back in her funny English. For the first time in her life, Caitriona had a friend of her own age.

'My mother, she would like to have you for a student, in our house in France,' whispered Aimée.

'I'd love to come,' Caitriona whispered back.

'But your father, he say no,' continued Aimée. 'He say he have no money. It is a pity, no?'

Caitriona glanced at the other cart, ahead of them. Her father was sitting there, slumped over — not humming or singing, just staring at the road ahead. He looked so downcast that Caitriona wanted to hug him, to take the sad look out of his eyes. She knew how proud he was of her singing, and how disappointed that he could not give her the chance to become a singer.

She turned to Aimée. 'Do you know,' she said, 'I think I might be able to find the money.'

All the way up the hill, the two girls talked about Malachy and his purse of gold. Aimée had a new idea.

'I think he perhaps interred it at Drumshee,' she said. 'He was at Drumshee when he write the book, not at Kilfenora.'

'You might be right,' said Caitriona, doubtfully. 'I hadn't thought of that. But then where do we start from — to measure the fifty-five paces, I mean?'

'When I come to Drumshee, I will see,' said Aimée confidently.

Caitriona had been afraid of what her stepmother would say about another French guest; and as soon as she and Aimée were upstairs in her bedroom, Caitriona could hear the angry hiss of Ann's voice. Resolutely she began to talk to Aimée at the top of her voice. I won't listen, she thought. Let Da deal with her. After all, he married her.

When they came downstairs, Ann seemed re-signed; she was bustling about putting the meal on the table. Aimée, like her brother, had charming manners, and soon everyone was sitting around the table, eating potatoes and cabbage and boiled bacon and chattering away. Aimée had a look at the little book in the lead box, and Caitriona pointed out the strange shape at the bottom of the cross. Serge and Caitriona, interrupting each other in their excite-ment, told Aimée the story of how the souterrain had been discovered; and after the meal was finished, everyone went up to have a look at it.

While Caitriona had been at Liscannor, Serge had

finished cleaning the souterrain. He had even given the walls a coat of whitewash and fixed some shelves to one of the soundest walls. The ancient pots stood empty beneath the shelves, and it really did look like a very nice storeroom.

'It's good enough for a bedroom,' said Tom. 'You can have this for your bedroom, Michael. Would you like that?'

Michael nodded his little head. 'Me and Bess,' he said. 'Bess is 'llowed in here. She sleep with me.'

'Isn't Bess lovely!' said Aimée. 'I think she is the nicest dog that I have ever met. I like very much the way she twists in circles and beats her tail and smiles at you. I wish I had a dog like that. I have always wanted a dog, and now my mother says that I may.'

'She's the nicest dog in the world,' said Caitriona. She knelt down on the ground, put her arms around Bess's neck and whispered in her ear.

'What are you saying to her?' asked Serge with an amused smile.

'I'm just telling her I'll keep my promise to her,' said Caitriona, getting to her feet.

After everyone had admired the souterrain, Ann went off to put Michael to bed, Tom went to check on the cattle, and Serge and Aimée and Caitriona were left alone outside the souterrain. Aimée's eyes were thoughtful.

'You remember our conversation, Caitriona, about the fifty-five paces? Why do we not start here? This is where the book was found. It might be fifty-five paces from here.'

Serge and Caitriona looked at each other with hope dawning in their eyes.

'I never thought of that,' said Serge. 'You are a clever little one, Aimée! Let's try it. We will each take a different direction. I will go west.'

'I go north, then,' said Aimée.

Caitriona paused. She looked around her. It suddenly seemed as if something desperately important hung on her choice. 'I'll go east,' she said finally. 'I'll go towards St Brigid's shrine.'

'Remember to take very long steps, the two of you,' warned Serge. 'Malachy was a man, so his pace might be longer than yours. When you reach fifty-five, mark the spot with a stick.'

Carefully Caitriona started to count, stretching her legs as far as she could. When she got to fifty, she realised that she was coming near the little shrine; and when she reached fifty-five, she was right beside it. She knelt down and stayed there, very still, until Aimée and Serge came over to find out what was keeping her.

Caitriona looked up at them. Her throat seemed to have swelled so that she could hardly find her voice, but finally she said huskily: 'It's wedge-shaped. The shrine is shaped like a wedge.'

Aimée looked puzzled. Unlike Caitriona, she had not pored over Malachy's picture of the cross for hours on end. Serge, however, had, and he understood immediately.

'Lift out the statue, Caitriona,' he said urgently.

Carefully Caitriona lifted out the statue of St Brigid and placed it on the grass. There was a small slab of stone under the statue. Serge leaned over and prised it up. Under the flagstone was a little hollow, and there in the centre of it was a leather purse. It was old and mouldy, and it almost fell apart when Caitriona picked it up, but it still held its contents.

Caitriona turned it upside-down and poured the golden coins into her lap. The other two waited while she counted them. When she had finished, she looked up with shining eyes.

'Twenty pieces of gold,' she said. 'Will that be enough for me to be trained as a singer?'

'That will be plenty,' Serge assured her.

'I cannot believe it!' cried Aimée, jumping up and down with excitement. 'You shall come back with us! You can share my bedroom. Serge, are you not pleased?'

Serge smiled. 'Yes,' he said softly. He stretched out his hand and squeezed Caitriona's, then dropped it as he saw Aimée's knowing smile.

Caitriona sat very still. Finally she got to her feet.

'Serge,' she said, 'will you take Aimée back to the house? I want to go and talk to Da.'

Tom was milking the cows, down in the Rough Field. Caitriona could hear him singing as she came down. She smiled to herself. He always said that the better the song, the better the milk, and it almost seemed as if he were right; certainly the cows always milked well for him and for Caitriona, but they held back a lot of the milk when Ann milked them.

Just before climbing the wall to cross the lane, Caitriona stopped. All the excitement seemed to drain out of her.

Going to France meant leaving her father, leaving Michael, leaving Drumshee; and suddenly she was not sure whether she wanted to.

She stood very still for a long time — so still that a fox, crossing from the Isle of Maain, passed quite close beside her.

Perhaps she could ask her father what she should do?

She shook her head. The decision had to be hers. She knew that. Tom would want her to stay at home, but he wouldn't stop her going away if she wanted it badly enough.

Caitriona looked up the lane, towards the Isle of Maain, and then down it towards Inchovea Castle. My life's like that lane, she thought; I have to choose to go one way or the other. France would mean training and the chance to succeed; but it would also mean loneliness, and perhaps failure.

As she stood there, she felt courage rise warmly inside her, and she nodded her head. Her decision was made. She put one hand on the wall, jumped over it lightly, and walked down the lane into the Rough Field.

'Da,' she said. 'You'll never guess what's happened. It's the most wonderful thing in the world.'

Her father stared at her, and the song died on his lips. 'You don't mean ...' he said.

Caitriona nodded her head firmly. 'Yes, I do,' she said. 'I've found that purse of gold. It was hidden in the shrine. Aimée got the idea that we should go fifty-five paces from the entrance to the souterrain, and then I noticed that the shape of the shrine is the same as the wedge-shape on the cross at Kilfenora, so we looked there. It was under the stone beneath the statue. Count it, Da. Will it be enough?'

Tom counted the gold coins slowly. 'It should be enough,' he said. He looked at the money thoughtfully, and then at Caitriona. 'I'll keep my promise to you,' he said quietly. 'You found the gold, so it's yours. The price of that book will be enough to keep the rest of us safe from any problems about the rent. But are you sure you want to go? It's a long way, and we don't know too much about these French people ....'

'You know Serge,' said Caitriona hotly. All traces of doubt had vanished from her mind; she was blazing with eagerness to start her new life. 'Remember, I'm nearly thirteen,' she said. 'I'd probably be going out to service in a big house soon, doing other people's housework. I'd be better off singing than doing that. You were the one who told me I should never waste the gift that God gave me. It wouldn't be much good singing while I was scrubbing floors.'

Her father tried to smile. 'Well, I suppose you haven't much of a gift for scrubbing floors, from all I hear,' he said. 'But I'm going to miss you, you know.'

'I know,' said Caitriona. She had to choke back a sob before she said it, but she was determined to be cheerful and confident. 'I'm going to miss you, too, and Michael and Ma, but I can come over and see you from time to time. Serge's uncle comes to Ireland twice every year, and I'm sure I could come with him.'

'Well, that's true,' said Tom, beginning to cheer up. 'And when you're singing in Paris, I'll come over and listen to you. Now let's get back up to the house and tell them the news.'

'There's one more thing,' said Caitriona, quickly. 'I want to take Bess. You know she's my dog, and I'd be miserable without her and she'd be miserable without me.'

'And what's Madame Dupont going to say to that?'

'Oh, she'll agree,' said Caitriona confidently. 'Serge and Aimée both love Bess.'

'Well, you know best,' said Tom. 'Now, who's going to tell your Ma, you or me?'

However, there was no need for either of them to say anything. Aimée and Serge had already broken the news, and Ann was bustling around the room in great excitement, making a cake and getting out some of her most delicious blackberry jam.

Caitriona began to help her — willingly, for once. This is the best thing for both of us, she thought. We've never really got on, and it's as much my fault as hers.

'Ma,' she said. 'Do you think I might need a new gown? '

Her stepmother's face brightened. Ann loved clothes, and always dressed very well.

'We'll all go to Galway tomorrow, Tom,' she said. 'We'll get Caitriona her clothes for going away, and we can see about selling that old book they found.'

'Well, if we get enough for it, we'll all get ourselves some new clothes,' said Tom. 'But I think it would be best if Serge stayed at home. I wouldn't like him to be spotted. Aimée can come. No one takes any notice of girls — it's soldiers they're looking for.'

'I'll look after the cows,' promised Serge. 'And I'll have the potatoes boiling by the time you come back.'

'And I will help Caitriona to choose a gown in the latest fashion from Paris!' said Aimée.

# CHAPTER FIFTEEN

The first thing they bought in Galway the next day was a trunk for Caitriona's clothes. Once this was done, Tom went off to see whether he could sell the Psalter of King David for a good price, and the others went into a Ladies' Millinery and did not come out for nearly three hours. Caitriona was quite frightened by the amount of clothes that they bought, but Ann was determined that she should not lack for anything.

'Madame Dupont isn't asking too much for your keep, and the lessons are quite cheap,' she said privately to Caitriona, while Aimée was examining the sprigged muslins. 'You must have some pretty gowns and some respectable shifts.'

In the end they settled on three linen shifts to be worn under dresses; two very fashionable white muslin dresses, softly gathered at the waist, with short sleeves and rounded necks; and, best of all, a beautiful morning robe. It was of creamy Irish linen, covered with trailing sprays of roses in pink and green, and it had a petticoat of shell-pink poplin; the robe was gathered at the back of the waist, and was longer at the back than at the front, so it gave the impression of having a slight train.

Caitriona had never in her life seen anything as exquisite as her new morning robe, and even Aimée could not stop admiring it.

'You can wear that when you sing in competitions,'

she said. 'Maman always likes her pupils to go to competitions, and it is necessary that you look your best for these. But you will need some satin shoes to wear with it, not these leather shoes.'

Caitriona gave a despairing look at her step-mother, but Ann was nodding and smiling.

'Yes,' she said, 'you're quite right, Aimée. Do you think they should be pink satin or white?'

'We will essay — no, I mean try — both,' said Aimée.

In the end they chose a pair of dark green satin shoes, the exact shade of the leaves on the gown, and added a small satin purse of the same green and a pair of rose-coloured satin gloves. When Caitriona looked in the mirror, she hardly recognised herself. She looked and looked, while Ann was over at the counter paying; and then she nodded at her reflection, just as if she were reassuring a stranger.

Yes, Caitriona said to herself, I can see that elegant figure as a famous singer on the stage in Paris.

It was all going to end well, she knew. The future seemed to pass in front of her, shadowy, but clearly visible in the smoky glass of the mirror. The sad farewells; the sea voyage, with Bess at her side; the arrival at the neat home outside Paris; the letters home; the years of hard work, the practising over and over again, the continual striving for perfection — and then, at last, success. She saw herself, grown up and elegant, and beside her a handsome young French officer, looking remarkably like Serge .... Caitriona blushed and turned hastily back to Aimée, who was still admiring the beautiful morning robe.

On the way back to Drumshee, they were all excited. Even Tom seemed to have put aside his sadness about Caitriona leaving; he sang every song he knew, and got the girls to sing with him, and the journey seemed shorter than it had ever been before. As the cart turned in at the gates, they were still singing; but then Caitriona stopped.

'Hush,' she said. 'Something's wrong. Bess is barking.'

Tom got down from the cart to close the gates, and stood listening.

'Probably a fox,' he said.

'No, it's not,' said Caitriona. 'I know the way Bess barks when a fox comes. This is different.' Hurriedly she hitched her dress up under her sash and climbed down over the wheel of the cart .

'Something's wrong,' she said, and began running up the avenue as fast as she could go.

'Caitriona, wait!' shouted her father, but she ignored him. On the ground she could see the prints of dozens of horseshoes; riders had come up the avenue not long before. Her heart was cold with dread, but she ran on up the steep slope, never pausing to draw breath.

Bess was still barking furiously, and Caitriona could hear voices, strange voices. A moment later she could make out some words — English words. She rounded the gable end of the cottage, and then stopped.

In front of the cottage was a crowd of soldiers — English soldiers in red coats, carrying muskets with fixed bayonets. And guarding the cottage door was gallant little Bess, barking with all the fury her small body was capable of, and making little dashes at any soldier who came within reach.

'Stick your bayonet into it!' shouted the sergeant.

'Don't you touch my dog!' screamed Caitriona. Reckless with desperation, she dashed in front of the soldiers, kicked aside the musket with its wickedly sharp bayonet, and picked up Bess. Without a tremor of fear, she faced the soldiers, her cheeks blazing scarlet and the dog in her arms.

'Don't you dare touch my dog!' she cried again.

Tom McMahon came running around the house, and immediately the muskets were lifted towards him. He stopped instantly and eyed them cautiously.

'You speak English?' asked the sergeant.

Tom hesitated, and then nodded. Most people around knew that he could speak English. It would serve no purpose to lie.

'Well,' continued the sergeant, 'we've heard that you're hiding someone here. Is this true?'

At that moment Ann came around the corner of the house, leading the horse. Aimée sat on the cart, holding the sleepy Michael on her lap. Caitriona held her breath. She knew her stepmother had heard the question; she could see how white her face was.

Tom, however, remained calm. He shook his head with an air of puzzlement.

'Who would we be hiding?' he said. 'There's just myself and the missus, and the two girls and the little fellow.'

Pray God he doesn't ask Aimée anything, thought Caitriona. He'll hear her French accent straight away.

Aimée, however, had obviously thought of that for herself: she climbed down from the cart, buried her face in Ann's shawl, and began to cry.

That's a good idea, thought Caitriona with a flash of admiration. If that English sergeant asks her anything, she can just go on crying. He won't take much notice of her. She's so small that she looks much younger than I am, really.

'Don't lie to me!' the sergeant snapped. 'We know you've had someone staying here.'

Tom's face cleared. 'Oh, you mean the lad, Patrick,' he said confidently. 'My cousin's lad. He's gone home.'

'Oh, really,' sneered the man. 'That's convenient. Just when we wanted to talk to him. And where would he be from, then?' Quickly he swung round on Caitriona. 'You tell me — you had plenty to say for yourself a minute ago. Where did this lad, Patrick, come from?'

Caitriona held Bess a little closer and eyed the sergeant defiantly.

'From the north of Ireland,' she said clearly.

'Ah,' said the sergeant, with a triumphant air. 'That's what we heard. Now stand aside,' he said roughly. 'We must search the house.'

'Stand back, Caitriona,' said Tom quietly. With a heavy heart, Caitriona obeyed. There were a dozen heavily-armed men there; she could not stop them, and her father would only get killed if he tried.

As the soldiers passed, Bess growled again, and one of the men lifted his musket threateningly.

'Be quiet, Bess,' said Caitriona. 'Don't worry. Nobody but a coward would try to harm a little dog like you.'

The soldier pushed by roughly, jostling Caitriona against the door-frame. She eyed him steadily and did not wince.

'You come with us,' the sergeant ordered Tom. 'Show us around. We'll soon see if you're telling the truth. You stay here,' he added, to one of the soldiers. 'Keep an eye on the girl and the woman and the two children. The rest of you, come with me. He may be armed.'

They were not gone long. There were only three rooms downstairs in the cottage, and Caitriona's bedroom in the loft. She could hear the soldiers going from room to room, knocking over furniture, pulling presses open and kicking iron pots aside. When they came back outside, Caitriona saw that her father's face was bruised and swollen. She closed her lips firmly and avoided his eyes.

'Take him with you to search the cabins and around the fields,' shouted the sergeant. 'I'll stay here.'

Silently Tom led the men into the cow cabin.

The sergeant eyed Ann McMahon appraisingly. She was even whiter now; she had seen what they had done to her husband. She'll tell them, thought Caitriona. The sergeant will get it out of her.

The sergeant obviously thought so too. His voice was suddenly gentle and coaxing. 'You might as well tell us, Missus,' he said. 'We'll find him in the end, and it will be better for you if you tell us sooner rather than later.'

Don't tell them anything, the words screamed in Caitriona's mind, don't tell them anything! They're only guessing. They know nothing. They can prove nothing!

She clenched her hands, and then unclenched them. The sergeant was looking intently from her to Ann, trying to gauge their reactions. Caitriona began to stroke Bess, whispering soft baby-talk to her. I'll try Aimée's little game, she thought. No one has given her a second glance.

'Tell me!' The sergeant's voice had turned rough. 'Or it will be the worse for you — and for your children.'

There was an agonising silence. Then Ann McMahon lifted her head. 'I don't know what you're talking about. My husband told you: Patrick Carney left here yesterday. To tell you the truth, I wasn't sorry to see the back of him. He spent more time singing than he did working. He wasn't much use to us.'

The sergeant looked at her keenly, but she didn't flinch. Her colour had come back, and she looked almost indifferent.

Why, she's as brave as any of us, after all! thought Caitriona, and a rush of shame came over her at the thought of how she had despised her stepmother. In fact, she's braver; that was a threat to Michael, and she stood up to it.

The men were returning from their search of the outbuildings. One of them shook his head. The sergeant made an abrupt signal, and the soldiers mounted their horses, turned, and went galloping down the avenue.

No one spoke or moved until the sound of the horses' hoofs on the hard surface of the road came to their ears. That seemed to be a signal to them all. Tom made a move towards his wife; but Caitriona was quicker. Dropping Bess, she put her arms around her stepmother and kissed her cheek.

'Come inside and have something to drink, Ma,' she said shyly. 'You look tired out.'

'I'll do that,' said Tom, taking Michael. 'You go and tell the lad he's safe — for the moment, anyway.'

'But where is he?' asked Aimée, bewildered.

Caitriona looked at her father and smiled. He smiled back.

'Where would he be but in the souterrain?' he said. 'It was himself that said it would be a good place to hide. Go and get him, Caitriona. We must get you all away tonight, though — the sooner the better. It's a good job that I'm a rich man and have two horses; I'll harness the new horse, and we'll have you all on board ship by midnight. Those men have gone towards Ennis, and we'll be going in the opposite direction. They never thought of the French at all; there must be more trouble going on in the north, and they thought the lad had come down here to organise us all!' He turned to Ann. 'You were the one who convinced them, Ann — you spoke up so well. I never knew you were so good at telling lies!'

Ann laughed a little shakily. She returned Caitriona's kiss, and then gave her a little push. 'Go to him,' she said softly. 'He'll be waiting for you. Aimée, you come and help me.'

Caitriona ran up towards the fort, with Bess at her heels. He must be there, she thought, suddenly frightened. What will I do if he's not there?

She looked cautiously all around, then raised the flagstone. There was not a sound from the souterrain. Hesitantly Caitriona began to move down the steps, her outstretched arms feeling the walls on either side. At the bottom of the steps she paused. 'Serge?' she said uncertainly, into the darkness.

Then she was in Serge's arms, and he was kissing her.

After a few moments he let her go, and she moved back, glad that the darkness prevented him from seeing how much she was blushing. Serge bent down to stroke Bess.

'I should be kissing Bess, as well as you,' he said softly. 'Without her, they would have caught me. All the time, as I ran behind the house and up to the *cathair*, I could hear her barking at them. She kept them busy while I lifted the stone and climbed down here. Bess is a very brave little dog. I am glad she will come to France with us. My mother would have welcomed her anyway, for your sake, but now she will welcome her even more, because she saved my life.'

'The soldiers are gone,' Caitriona said. 'You can come up now.' She felt suddenly shy; she didn't know what to say to Serge.

He took her hand, and she followed him confidently up the steep steps. Hand in hand, they wandered through the *cathair*; the moon was coming up, and the ancient enclosure was lit with a pale silver glow.

So I was right, thought Caitriona, when I saw Serge and me together in the mirror ....

They stopped beside the old ash tree which hid the sacred shrine of Saint Brigid, where Malachy's golden secret had waited for them for hundreds of years. Below, in the yard, they could see Tom harnessing the horse to the heavy wooden cart, getting ready to set off for the ship which would carry Caitriona, Serge and Bess to far-off France — and a new life.

But none of us will ever forget Drumshee, Caitriona thought. That's where it all began.

# ALSO BY CORA HARRISON

## *Nuala and her Secret Wolf*
**Drumshee Timeline Series Book 1**

Fergus, an orphaned wolf-cub, is Nuala's secret —
and her dearest friend.

Everyone in her Iron Age world hates and fears
wolves, and she knows that if her father finds Fergus
he will kill him. So she feeds him, plays with him
and trains him to track and herd — all in secret.

But there is danger, and not only for Fergus.
Cattle-raiders are watching the fort —
and their leader wants Nuala for his bride.

Can Fergus save Nuala and her family?

Warm, fast-paced, rich in historical detail,
*Nuala and her Secret Wolf* is a story to enchant
animal-lovers everywhere.

ISBN 0-86327-585-0

# *The Secret of the Seven Crosses*
## Drumshee Timeline Series Book 2

When Malachy joined the monks at Kilfenora Abbey,
he thought the abbey offered everything he wanted
— safety from the raiders who are terrifying
thirteenth-century Ireland, new friends,
beautiful books for him to copy.
But then he starts to realise that
the abbey has its secrets ....

What does the mysterious pattern
in the herb-garden mean?

Who is trying to steal the ancient
Psalter of King David?

And what has become of
the long-lost treasure of Kilfenora?

With the help of his friend Rory, Rory's sister Mary,
and a wonderful Siamese cat, Malachy sets out to
discover the secret of Kilfenora —
before someone else gets there first.

ISBN 0-86327-616-4

# *The Secret of Drumshee Castle*
## Drumshee Timeline Series Book 3

*'With a sudden shock, Grace realised:
She hates me enough to kill me ....'*

Grace is an orphan, living at Drumshee Castle in the
time of Queen Elizabeth I. She thinks she can survive
anything as long as she has her pony, Golden Dawn.

But Grace's cruel aunt and uncle want her land,
and they are plotting to get rid of her — and one night,
their carefully-laid plans turn into action.

Helped by her powerful cousin Brendan, her foster-
brother Enda, and her beloved Golden Dawn,
Grace escapes and sets out in search of safety and
justice. But even amidst the splendour
of Queen Elizabeth's court,
she longs for the peaceful hills of Drumshee.

Will she ever be able to return?

ISBN 0-86327-632-6

# *The Famine Secret*
## Drumshee Timeline Series Book 5

Fiona dreams of being a famous writer; her twin
sister Deirdre wants to learn how to make lace.
But it's 1847 at Drumshee:
blight has withered the potatoes,
the terrible black fever has killed the twins' parents,
and poverty finally drives the girls and their brothers
into the workhouse.

In order to survive, the four children have to fight
against hunger, fever, and the cruel Matron's greed;
but they are determined that Fiona's wonderful
imagination and Deirdre's practical common sense
will come up with a way for them to escape.

And they know that if they do, their beloved home
will be waiting to welcome them back —
because once again, Drumshee is hiding a secret ....

ISBN 0-86327-649-0

*All titles in the Drumshee Timeline Series are available from:*

WOLFHOUND PRESS
68 Mountjoy Square
Dublin 1
Tel: (+353 1) 874 0354          Fax: (+353 1) 872 0207